30.00

GIFTS

Philip and Muriel Berman Edition

The
Auth or's
Work shop

THE JEWISH PUBLICATION SOCIETY OF AMERICA
PHILADELPHIA · NEW YORK · JERUSALEM
5745 · 1985

ISAAC BASHEVIS SINGER

GIFTS

Copyright © 1985 by Isaac Bashevis Singer
First edition
Manufactured in the United States of America

Library of Congress Cataloging in Publication Data

Singer, Isaac Bashevis, 1904–
   Gifts.
   (The Author's workshop)
   Contents: The trap — The pocket remembered —
The smuggler — [etc.]
     1. Singer, Isaac Bashevis, 1904–   — Translations,
English.   I. Title.   II. Series.
PJ5129.S49A2   1984   839.0933   84–25095
ISBN 0–8276–0249–9

Designed by ADRIANNE ONDERDONK DUDDEN

The Author's Workshop is a series of limited first editions by significant American writers who are choosing to address a Jewish audience—some for the first time. Each volume represents a unique publishing story: Concentrating on imaginative writing, it includes works in progress as well as recent works that have never been printed until now or have not previously appeared in book form. Each volume begins with an original autobiographical introduction. The book as a whole will not again be available to the public. These limited editions are conceived primarily for the members of the Jewish Publication Society, who have been supporting innovative Jewish publishing in America for almost one hundred years.

Probably best known for its Bible translations, JPS has taken the initiative in developing all aspects of Jewish culture—religion, art, poetry, literature in translation, history, legend, pioneering scholarship and classics of Jewish thought, both modern and time-honored. Continuing its original mandate to shape the growth of Jewish culture in its American form, JPS is now aware of a new Jewish audience, sophisticated enough to confront its history and resources in a creative way. *The Author's Workshop* is the first of several series which are planned to stimulate the definition and growth of Jewish culture in America by focusing on its imaginative writers. As recently as twenty years ago, it was rare that someone not brought up as a Jew would address a secular Jewish audience, such as is now in resurgence in America as well as in Israel.

Just as each generation of artists in a free society has to decide for itself what painting or poetry should be, each generation of Jewish artists defines its Jewishness. What counts in both art and Judaism is not only spectacular beginnings but also the power of renewal. Today, what is missing is not the authors but the context in which Jewish books can receive the care and devotion they deserve. JPS, in establishing these new series of books to nurture a Jewish context, is helping to create a sense of community to inspire authors as well as readers. Jewish memory has been rejuvenated with JPS translations; in the same tradition, *The Author's Workshop* is a pioneering presentation of contemporary Jewish authors.

Gifts by I. B. Singer shows the latest work by this trailblazer in twentieth-century Jewish culture. These previously unprinted stories were chosen for their special Jewish interest from among Mr. Singer's recent writings. At least half the contents of *Gifts* will not appear in his next full collection of stories; in addition, the title story, "Gifts," is printed in its original Yiddish. The introduction to this volume demonstrates the continuity of I. B. Singer's vision, which survives the most unimaginable kind of uprooting a writer must face.

CONTENTS

GIFTS

AUTHOR'S INTRODUCTION

I have lived through a number of epochs in Jewish history. I was brought up in a home where the old Jewish faith burned brightly. Ours was a house of Torah and holy books. Other children had toys; I played with the volumes in my father's library. I began to write before I even knew the alphabet. I took my father's pen, dipped it in ink, and started to scribble. The Sabbath was an ordeal for me, because on that day writing is forbidden.

My father moved to Warsaw when I was still very young, and there a second epoch began for me: the age of the Enlightenment. My brother, I. J. Singer, who later wrote *The Brothers Ashkenazi*, was at that time a rationalist; it was not in his nature to hide his opinions. He spoke frankly to my parents, advancing with great clarity and precision all the arguments that the rationalists—from Spinoza to Max Nordau—had brought against religion. Though I was still a child, I listened attentively. Fortunately, my parents did not lack answers. They replied with as much skill as my brother attacked. I recall my father saying, "Well, who created the world? You? Who made the sky, the stars, the sun, the moon, man, the animals?" My brother's answer was that everything had evolved. He mentioned Darwin. "But," my mother wanted to know, "how can a creature with eyes, ears, lungs, and a brain evolve from earth and water?" My father used to say, "You can spatter ink but it won't write a letter by itself." My brother never had an answer for this; as yet none has been found.

My parents attempted to further strengthen the case for faith by constantly telling stories of imps, ghosts, and dybbuks and of the miraculous feats of famous rabbis. Some of these events they themselves had witnessed, and I knew that they were not liars. My grandfather, the Rabbi of Bilgoray, had once been visited by an old man, a fortune teller, who had been able to read the text of a closed book; whatever page my grandfather touched with his finger, the fortune teller could recite. I later used this incident in a story of mine, "The Jew of Babylon," which has not yet been translated. My mother knew of a house inhabited by a poltergeist. Indeed, I can truthfully say that by the time I was seven or eight I was already acquainted with all the strange facts that are to be found in the books of Conan Doyle, Sir Oliver Lodge, Gourney and Myers, Flammarion and Professor Rhine. In our home the most pressing questions were the eternal ones; there the cosmic riddles were not theoretical but actual. I began to read in *The Guide of the Perplexed* and *The Kuzari*, even in the Cabalistic literature, at an early age. But nevertheless, despite my studies, I remained a child and played joyfully with other children. At Cheder I astounded my fellow students with fantastic stories. I told them once that my father was a king and with such convincing detail that they believed me.

When the first World War broke out, I experienced all the social evils of the period. I saw the men on our street marching off to war, leaving behind them sobbing women and hungry children. Men from the very house I lived in were taken. In his debates with my brother, my father argued, "You keep on talking about reason and logic. What logic is there to this war? How does it happen that learned men and teachers assist in the manufacture of bombs and guns to destroy innocent people?" Again my brother had no answer. He himself was drafted. During the short time that he was a recruit, he endured every kind of humiliation. The Russian and Polish recruits accused him of murdering Jesus, poisoning wells, using Christian blood for matzohs, and spying for the Germans. In the barracks reason was bankrupt. My high-minded brother fled to Warsaw and hid in the studio of a sculptor. I used to carry food to him there.

No. The world that was revealed to me was not rational. One could as easily question the validity of reason as the existence of God. In my own spirit, there was chaos. I suffered from morbid dreams and hallucinations. I had wildly erotic fantasies. Hungry children, filthy beggars, refugees sleeping in the streets, wagons of wounded soldiers did not arouse admiration in me for human or divine reason. The spectacle of a cat pouncing on a mouse made me sick and rebellious. Neither human reason nor God's mercy seemed to be certain. I found both filled with contradictions. My brother still clung to the hope that in the end reason would be victorious. But young though I was I knew that the worship of reason was as idolatrous as bowing down to a graven image. As yet I had not read the modern philosophers, but I had come to the conclusion by myself that reason leads to antinomies when it deals with time, space, and causality; it could deal no better with these than with the *ultimate problem*, the problem of evil.

In 1917 my mother took me and one of my younger brothers to Bilgoray, which was being occupied by the Austrians. Kerensky's revolution had occurred and was regarded as the victory of reason, but soon came the October Revolution and the pogroms in the Ukraine. Bilgoray had just endured a cholera epidemic. The town had lost a third of its inhabitants. Some of my relatives had been stricken. The gruesome tales of that pestilence are still fresh in my memory.

Bilgoray had no railroad and was surrounded by forests, and there the Jewish traditions of a hundred years before were still very much alive. I had already become acquainted with the modern Hebrew and Yiddish literature. The writers of both languages were under the influence of the Enlightenment. These authors wanted the Jew to step out of his old-fashioned gaberdine and become European. Their doctrines were rationalistic, liberal, humanistic. But to me such ideas seemed already obsolete. The overthrowing of one regime and the replacing of it with another did not seem to me to be the crux of the matter. The problem was creation itself. I felt that I must achieve some sort of solution of the puzzle or perish myself.

While in Bilgoray I became acquainted with the literature of other nations. I read in translation Tolstoy, Dostoevsky, Gogol, Heine, Goethe, Flaubert, Maupassant. I read Jack London's *The Call of the Wild* and the stories of Edgar Allan Poe, all in Yiddish. It was at this time also that I first studied Spinoza's *Ethics* in a German translation. I pored over each page as though it were a part of the Talmud. Some of the axioms, definitions, and theorems I still remember by heart. I am now able to see the defects and hiatuses in Spinoza's system, but my reading of the *Ethics* had a great effect on me. My story "The Spinoza of Market Street" is rooted in this period. Later I read a history of philosophy and Hume, Kant, Schopenhauer, and Nietzsche. My childish hope was to discover the truth, and through the discovery to give sense and substance to my life. But finally my conclusion was that the power of philosophy lay in its attack upon reason, not in the building of systems. None of the systems could be taken seriously; they did not help one to manage one's life. The human intellect confronted existence, and existence stubbornly refused to be systematized. I myself was the insulted and shamed human intellect. Many times I contemplated suicide because of my intellectual impotence.

All these storms took place inside me. On the outside I was just a Chassidic boy who studied the Gemara, prayed three times a day, put on phylacteries. But the people of the town were suspicious anyway. They considered me an exotic plant. I saw with grief and sometimes envy how other boys my age made peace somehow with this world and its troubles. I lacked their humility.

At that time I began to write in Hebrew. So perturbed was my spirit that I expected my pen to at least partially express my rage. But I saw with shame that nothing issued but banal and thrashed-about phrases, similar to those I read in other books and which I criticized severely. I felt as if a devil or imp held on to my pen and inhibited it. A mysterious power did not let me reveal my inner self. After many trials I decided it was the fault of the Hebrew language. Hebrew was near to me, but it was not my mother language. While writing, I kept on searching in my memory for words and phrases from the Bible, the Mishnah, and the later literature; in addition, each Hebrew word dragged after itself a whole chain of associations. I came to the conclusion that writing in Yiddish would be easier. But I soon found that this was not so. I still had not lost my inhibitions. Satan did not allow me to express my individuality. Despite myself, I imitated Knut Hamsun, Turgenev, and even lesser writers. Every creator painfully experiences the chasm between his inner vision and its ultimate expression. This chasm is never completely bridged. We all have the conviction, perhaps illusory, that we have much more to say than appears on the paper.

I began an investigation of the techniques of literature. What, I asked myself, makes Tolstoy and Dostoevsky so great? Is it the theme, the style, or the construction? My brother, I. J. Singer, had left Poland and gone to Russia. He was residing in Kiev, where he wrote for the Yiddish press, and had already published his story "Pearls." One day he showed up in Bilgoray to spend the day. As a writer he had "already arrived." I had sufficient character not to show him my manuscripts. I knew that I had to find my way by myself.

Some time thereafter, I went to live in Warsaw, which was then the center of Yiddish culture in Poland. It was in the early twenties. I had not yet published anything. At that time my brother was a friend of the famous Perez Markish, who was later liquidated by Stalin. Other members of his literary circle were Melechavitch, Uri Zvi Greenberg, today a famous Hebrew poet, and American Yiddish writers like Joseph Opatoshu, who came on visits to Warsaw. My brother was co-editor of the *Literarische Blatter*, and I got a job there as a proofreader. A spirit of revolution permeated the new Yiddish literature: Markish wrote in the style of Mayakovsky. But Aleksandr Blok, the Russian poet, author of the poem "Twelve," was the most beloved writer of that group. This coterie preached that classic and academic literature was bankrupt and spoke of a new time, a new period, a new style.

I was afraid to set myself against writers who were all well recognized, although I saw that their art was new in neither spirit nor style. They had merely dressed up the old clichés in red clothing. All they did was juggle words. Even a young boy like me, from the provinces, found the doctrine that the Bolshevist revolution would do away with all evil incredibly naïve. The Jewish situation in Poland was especially bad. The Polish people—the people themselves, not merely the regime—had never come to terms with the Jews. The Jews had built a separate society in Poland and had their own faith, language, holidays, and even political aspirations. We Jews were both citizens and aliens. My father, for example, could speak no Polish. I myself spoke Polish with an accent. Though my ancestors had lived in Poland for six hundred years, we were still strangers. No revolution could unite these two communities which were so profoundly separated. Communism and Zionism, the two ideals which split the Jews of Poland, were both completely alien to the Polish people. I do not mean to imply by this that I had remarkable prescience, but I saw clearly that the Jews were living on a volcano. In my bitterness I spoke about the coming catastrophe, but those around me were puffed up with optimism, rationalism, and Red dogmatism.

My brother soon freed himself of revolutionary illusions, but he nonetheless kept his belief in reason. He still thought that through evolution and progress, man would slowly see his mistakes and correct them. We had many discussions. In a sense, I had taken over the position of my parents. I tried mercilessly to destroy his humanistic optimism. I regret now that I did this, because what did I have to offer? My parents at least advocated religion. Mine was only a negative philosophy. My brother was always tolerant and deeply sympathetic to me, but I was rebellious and often insolent.

A new *Weltanschauung* which I find difficult to characterize began to develop in me. It was a kind of religious skepticism. There is a God, but He never reveals Himself; no one knows who He is or what His purpose is. There are an infinite number of universes, and even here, on this earth, powers exist of which we have no inkling, both stronger and weaker than Man. This system allowed for the possibility of angels and devils and for other beings which are and will remain forever unnamed. I had, in a curious way, combined the Ten Commandments, Humian philosophy, and the Cabalistic writing of Rabbi Moshe from Cordova and the Holy Isaac Luria, as well as the occultism of Flammarion, Sir Oliver Lodge, Sir William Crooks. This was, as one can see, a sort of kasha of mysticism, deism, and skepticism, well suited to my intellect and temperament. Instead of a concrete universe of facts, I saw a developing universe of potentialities. The thing-in-itself is pure potential. In the beginning was potentiality. What seem to be facts are really potentialities. God is the sum of all possibility. Time is the mechanism through which potentiality achieves sequence. The Cabala teaches that all worlds are created through the combination of letters. My own position was that the universe is a series of countless potentialities and combinations. I had already read Schopenhauer's *The World as Will and Idea* and so knew the Schopenhaurian view that the will is the thing-in-itself, the noumenon behind the phenomenon. But, to me, the basic substance of the world was potentiality seen as a whole.

I did not conceive of this as a philosophy for others, but strictly for myself. Somehow or other it made sense for me, but I didn't have the means or the need to systematize it and make it understandable to others. I would say that it was more a philosophy of art than of being.

God was for me an eternal belletrist. His main attribute was creativity. God was creativity, and what He created was made of the same stuff as He and shared His desire: to create again. I quoted to myself that passage from the Midrash which says God created and destroyed many worlds before he created this one. Like my brother and myself God threw His unsuccessful works into the wastebasket. The Flood, the destruction of Sodom, the wanderings of the Jews in the desert, the wars of Joshua—these were all episodes in a divine novel, full of suspense and adventure. Yes, God was a creator, and that which He created had a passion to create. Each atom, each molecule had creative needs and possibilities. The sun, the planets, the fixed stars, the whole cosmos seethed with creativity and creative fantasies. I could feel this turmoil within myself.

I availed myself of the doctrine of *zimzum*, that wonderful notion which is so important in the Cabala of Rabbi Isaac Luria. God, Isaac Luria says, is omnipotent, but had to diminish Himself and His light so that He could create. Such shrinking is the source of creation, not only in man but also in the Godhead. The evil host makes creation possible. God could not have His infinite works without the devil. Out of suffering creativity is born. The existence of pain in the world can be compared with a writer's suffering as he describes some dreadful scene which he lives through in his imagination. As he writes the author knows that his work is only fiction produced for his and his reader's enjoyment. Each man, each animal, exists only as clay in the hands of a creator, and is itself creative. We, ourselves, are the writer, the book, and the hero. The medieval philosophers expressed a similar idea when they said that God is Himself the knower, the known, and the knowledge.

I am not seeking here to create a new philosophy. All I desire to do is to describe a state of mind. Just as an artist hopes throughout his whole life to create the great and perfect work, so does God yearn throughout all eternity to perfect His creation. God is no static perfection, as Spinoza thought, but a limitless and unsatiated will for perfection. All His worlds are nothing more than stages and experiments in a divine laboratory. When I went to the Cheder as a boy and studied "Akdamoth," the poem for Pentecost, I was amazed by the verses in the poem which said that if all skies were parchment, all men writers, all blades of grass pens, and all oceans ink, these would still be insufficient to describe the mysteries of the Torah. That parable became my credo: The skies were indeed parchment, the grasses pens, and all men in fact writers. Everything that existed wrote, painted, sculpted, and sought for creative achievement.

Since the purpose of creation was creation, creativity was also the criterion of ethics and even of sociology. There was a place only for those social systems which could advance creativity. Freedom was nothing but the freedom to create. Since creativity required leisure, and some degree of wealth, men must create a system which would furnish the requisites to experiment.

Yes, God is a writer, and we are both the heroes and the readers. A novel written by the Lord cannot endure just for one short season. As heroes of God's novel we are all immortal. A great writer's work can be understood on many levels, and this implies that our existence has more than one meaning. We exist in body. We exist as symbols, as parables, and in many other ways. When the critics praise a writer they say that his hero is three-dimensional, but God's heroes have more than three dimensions. Their dimensions are numberless.

Good novels are often translated into many languages, and so is the novel called Life. Versions of this work are read on other planets, on other galaxies of the universe.

Apropos of the critics: Like all writers, the Almighty has His critics. We know that the angels have nothing but praise for His work. Three times a day they sing: Sublime! Perfect! Great! Excellent! But there must be some angry critics too. They complain: Your novel, God, is too long, too cruel. Too little love. Too much sex. . . . They advise cutting. How can a novel be good when three quarters of it is water? They find it inconsistent, sensational, antisocial,

cryptic, decadent, vulgar, pointless, melodramatic, impro-
vised, repetitious. About one quality we all agree: God's
novel has suspense. One keeps on reading it day and night.
The fear of death is nothing but the fear of having to close
God's book. We all want to go on with this serial forever.
The belief in survival has one explanation: We refuse to
have any interruptions in reading. As readers we are burning with a desire to know the events of the next chapter,
and the next, and the next. We try hard to find the formula
for God's best seller, but we are always wrong. The heavenly writer is full of surprises. All we can do is pray for a
happy ending. . . . But according to the Cabala, God's novel
will never end. The coming of the Messiah will be only the
beginning of a new volume. Resurrection will bring back
some characters the reader has already forgotten, but not
the writer. . . . What we call death is but a temporary pause
for purely literary reasons.

Suddenly my way in literature became clear to me: to
transform inhibition into a method of creativity, to recog-
nize in the inhibition a friendly power instead of a hostile
one—in the terms of the Cabala, to lift up the holy sparks
which had fallen from the sacred into the impure, from the
World of Emanations into the unclean host. Even though I
realized that this philosophy was nothing but my private
concoction, I considered it valid and useful as a basis for my
work. In the world of the artist, the teaching of Isaac Luria
is certainly true: The shadow is often the precursor of the
light; the devils and imps are temptations and challenges to
further achievement. The purpose of each fall is a new ris-
ing. Each occasion for sin can become an occasion for virtue.
Each passion, no matter how low, can become a ladder to
ascend.

Satan in Goray, which I wrote in 1932, was a product of this state of mind. The epoch of Sabbatai Zevi was for me a rare opportunity to express these thoughts in a symbolic way. This epoch was for me a lesson in both religion and creativity: One must learn from the inhibition, discover its higher purpose; one must neither ignore it completely nor submit to it. The inhibition in the broadest sense is always an indication of new potentialities. In almost all my later works, I try to show man's urge to create, to find what is new, unique, and to overcome the disturbances and barriers in his way.

Creativity is for me a very encompassing idea. I would say that everything which gives a man pleasure is creative and what causes him pain is an inhibition in his creative desire. Like Spinoza, I am a hedonist. Like the Cabalists, I believe that the principle of male and female exists not only in the lower worlds but also in the higher ones. The universal novel of creation, like the novel of an earthly writer, is finally a love story.

The Cabalists compared the unclean host with the female, and this comparison has deep significance. A male can bring out his semen quickly and in abundance, but the female demands time, patience, and a period of ripening. She is, if you want, the inhibition, but she is also the power which transmutes intention into deed. The Cabalists saw in God a division into the masculine and the feminine, which they called the Shechinah. God Himself must have time and space for His work. In His original form He is not perfect but ripens in infinite time. God, like the Universe, is expanding. Men can serve Him by creating within their narrow worlds, in their small way, conditions which will permit creativity for all—from the bee to man, from the microbe that sours our milk to the artist. The freedom to which we aspire should not be an end in itself. Its ultimate aim must be Man's boundless creativity.

God creates continuously, and continuous creation is Man's destiny, too. God, like the artist, is free. Like the artist's His work cannot be predetermined. Laws are aesthetic and ethical and therefore bound to change. Continual change is their very essence. Beauty is their purpose. God's fantasy is their limit. God, like the artist, never knows clearly what He will do and how His work will develop. Only the intention is clear: to bring out a masterpiece and to improve it all the time. I have once called God a struggling artist. This continual aspiration is what men call suffering. In this system emotions are not passive, as in Spinoza's philosophy. God Himself is emotion. God thinks and feels. Compassion and beauty are two of His endless attributes. In my novel *The Slave*, I have expressed this notion in these words:

> The summer night throbbed with joy; from all sides came music. Warm winds bore the smells of grain, fruit, and pine trees to him. Itself a Cabalistic book, the night was crowded with sacred names and symbols—mystery upon mystery. In the distance where sky and earth merged, lightning flashed, but no thunder followed. The stars looked like letters of the alphabet, vowel points, notes of music. Sparks flickered above the bare furrows. The world was a parchment scrawled with words and song. Every now and then Jacob heard a murmur in his ear as if some unseen being was whispering to him. He was surrounded by powers, some good, some evil, some cruel, some merciful, but each with its own nature and its own task to perform.

THE TRAP

"I tried to write," the woman said, "but first of all I'm not a writer. Secondly, even if I were a writer I couldn't write this story. The moment I begin—and I began a number of times—my fountain pen starts to make ugly smudges on the paper. I never learned how to type. They brought me up so that I have no skill for technical things. I cannot drive a car. I cannot change a fuse. Even to find the right channel on a television set is for me a problem."

The woman who said this to me had white hair and a young face without wrinkles. I had put her crutches in a corner. She sat in my apartment in a chair which I had purchased some time ago in an antique store.

She said, "My father and mother both came from rich homes. My maternal grandfather was actually a millionaire in Germany. He lost everything in the inflation after World War I. He was lucky; he died in Berlin long before Hitler came to power. My father came from Alsace. For some reason my father always warned me not to have anything to do with Jews who come from Russia. He used to say they aren't honest and they're all communists. If he had lived to see my husband he would have been surprised. I never met as violent an adversary of communism as he was. Boris was his name. He assured me many times that Roosevelt was a hidden Bolshevik and that he had an agreement with Stalin to deliver a half of Europe to him on a silver platter and even the United States. Boris's father was a Russian, a devout Christian, and a Slavophile. His wife, Boris's mother, was Jewish. She was a Hungarian. I did not know her. She was a classic beauty and completely eccentric. In their last years husband and wife did not talk to each other. When they wanted to communicate they sent notes to each other through the maid. I'm not going to bother you with too many details. I'll come right to the point.

"I met Boris in 1938 in a hotel in Lake Placid in the Adirondacks. My father had died in Dachau, where the Nazis had sent him. From grief my mother lost her mind, and she was placed in an insane asylum. Boris was a guest in the hotel and I was a chambermaid. I had come from Germany without a penny, and this was the only job I could get. Our matchmaker was Thomas Mann's novel *Buddenbrooks*. I came to make Boris's room and there the novel lay on the table. I was in love with that work. For a while I left the bed which I was making and began to leaf through the pages. Suddenly the door opened and Boris came in. He was twelve years older than I. I was then twenty-four and he was thirty-six. I'm not going to boast to you about my good looks. What you are seeing now is a ruin. The woman who sits here before you went through five operations. In one case I actually died. I stopped breathing some hours after the operation, and the night nurse without any ceremony covered my face with a sheet. Don't laugh. Those were the happiest moments I can remember. If death is actually as blissful as those minutes were, there's no reason to fear it."

"How were you revived?" I asked.

"Oh, the night nurse suddenly decided that she'd better notify the doctor. A number of physicians ran in and brought me back to life. What a miserable life! But all the wretchedness came later. I can never tell anything in a chronological order. I have no sense of time and have no recollection for the order of events. Do me a favor and bring me a glass of water."

"Yes, of course."

I brought the woman a glass of water, and I said, "I forgot to ask you your name. Is it a secret?"

"No secret. My name is Regina Kozlov. Kozlov is my husband's surname. My maiden name is Wertheim. I will try to make my story as short as possible.

"We stood in the hotel room and we both praised Thomas Mann. Boris was tall, straight, a handsome man; perhaps too handsome. I told him that he could have been a film actor, but even then I saw something in his eyes which frightened me. They had not one color but a few colors: blue, green, and even violet. They expressed a kind of stubbornness, severity, fanaticism. Why go on? We fell in love, as they say, at first sight, and two weeks later we got married right there in Lake Placid.

"Neither he nor I had any close relatives in America. He told me he had a sister in London who was married to an English aristocrat, some sir or lord. What did I care? I was absolutely alone in the world, without means, and here I got a husband who had received a law degree in Warsaw.

He told me that he had no patience to take a bar examination in the United States and that he made a living from business. 'What kind of business?' I asked him, and he said, 'Stocks and bonds.' After the Wall Street crash most stocks fell so low they became almost worthless, but at the end of the thirties they began to rise. Boris had brought with him to the United States quite a large sum of money, and in some five years he managed to double or triple his investments. In New York he had bought a large building for a pittance, and he sold it with a big profit. He had an apartment in Brooklyn Heights, stocks and bonds which may have been worth half a million dollars, and all he needed was a wife. 'How did it happen that the girls didn't grab you up till now?' I asked, and he said that many tried, but he never found anyone who pleased him. He said to me, 'I'm a serious man and to me marriage is a serious institution. I demand from a woman physical and spiritual beauty and strong moral values. When I take one look at someone I can see all her shortcomings, not only the actual but also the potential ones.'

"According to his talk, I was at least an angel, if not a goddess, and he had seen all this at first sight. It's a fact that he began to talk to me about marriage immediately in the room which I came to clean. To make it short, one day I was a chambermaid and a few days later I was engaged to become Mrs. Kozlov. The hotel was full of German Jews. The announcement created quite a sensation among them. They're not accustomed to such quick decisions. Mothers of marriageable daughters were bursting with envy. I must tell you a funny episode: The first or second day he asked me if I was a virgin and I told him yes, which was the truth. I added in a joke, 'A virgin with a certificate.' The moment I said these words Boris became tense and frightened. 'A certificate from whom?' he asked. 'From a doctor? What doctor? Here in America?' I assured him again and again that I was joking. 'Certificate' is a Yiddish expression that means one hundred percent. But I could see that he did not have the slightest sense of humor. It took me a long time to quiet him. I saw right away that one could not make a joke with Boris. If there was such a thing as a degree for humorlessness he would have gotten one *magna cum laude*. We got married at Lake Placid by a justice of the peace, and no one took part in the ceremony but two bailiffs who served as witnesses. Boris had a sister in London, but as far as I knew he didn't inform her of our marriage. After a while we went to New York, and my entire luggage consisted of one valise. Boris lived in a small apartment in a building without an elevator: two large half-empty rooms, a kitchen, and a little room which he called his office. It may sound funny to you but he had one narrow bed, one plate, one spoon, one knife, and one glass. I asked what he did when he had company, and he said, 'No one ever comes to me.' I asked him, 'Don't you have any friends?' and he said, 'There are no friends. My only friend is my broker.' It didn't take me long to realize I had married a man who was pathologically literal. He had a book where he kept a record of every cent he spent. Once when I walked with him on the street I found a penny on the sidewalk. I gave it to him for good luck, and he later wrote down the penny as income in his book. I'm not even sure that I should call him a miser. He later bought me clothes and jewelry. He planned to buy a house, but not until I became pregnant. I would say that he was extremely serious, and the slightest hint of a joke drove him into confusion. I read some time ago that they're building robots that think. If such robots are built they'll be just like Boris: accurate, precise, practical, and pragmatic. In the short time we spent together at Lake Placid it became clear he was a silent man. He only said what he had to say. I cannot to this day say why he was so delighted with *Buddenbrooks*, a work filled with humor: perhaps because extremes attract one another. This man could have lived out his life with two words, 'yes' and 'no.' I had made a tragic mistake, but I decided to make the best of it. I wanted to be a devoted wife and later a devoted mother. We both wanted children. I hoped the children would take after my family, not his.

"It was a terribly lonesome existence from the beginning. Boris awakened every day at seven o'clock to the second. He ate the same breakfast every morning. He suffered from an ulcer and the doctor had put him on a diet, which he followed rigorously. He went to bed exactly at ten. He never changed his single bed into a double bed, waiting for the time when he'd buy a house. We were living among Jews. The war had begun. Jewish boys and girls were collecting money for Palestine, but Boris told them he was an anti-Zionist. There were also some communists on our street, and they collected money for Birobidzhan and such similar fakes. When Boris heard the word 'communists' he became wild. He screamed that Russia was ruled by murderers and vampires. He said that his only hope was that Hitler would clean up the red swamp. For a Jew to put his hopes in Hitler was a terrible thing. The neighbors all stopped greeting me. There was even a rumor that neither of us was a Jew.

"When five months passed and I did not get pregnant, Boris demanded that I visit a doctor. This was a bitter pill for me. I was always shy, and it embarrassed me to be examined by a gynecologist. I told Boris it was too early to go to doctors, and he fell into a rage. The idea that someone could see things differently from the way he did made him furious. I went to a gynecologist, and he came to the conclusion that I was a hundred percent normal. The doctor suggested that it would be quite appropriate for my husband to be examined too. I told Boris, and he immediately made an appointment. He went through a multitude of tests, and it was established that he was sterile, not I.

"It was a blow for both of us. I let it slip out that perhaps we should adopt a child. Immediately, Boris became hysterical. He screamed that never in his life would he take into his house a bastard whose parents were criminals and who would grow up to be a criminal himself. He yelled so loudly I was afraid the neighbors would come running. I kept assuring him that I wouldn't adopt anyone against his will and he needn't create scandals, but when he fell into a rage he couldn't be quieted. I must say sometimes his screams were more welcomed than his silence.

"Actually, Boris carried on long telephone conversations with his broker. Sometimes they spoke for an hour, even longer. This broker was a private consultant, not a member of a brokerage firm. In all my married years I never met him. In the five years we lived together I couldn't make Boris go with me to a theater, a movie, or a concert. He was interested in nothing but money. I must tell you all this so that you'll understand what happened later. Please be patient."

"Yes, I'm patient," I said.

We rested for a few minutes, and the woman took a lozenge and a sip of water. I asked, "What kind of a married life was this?"

The woman's eyes lit up. "It's good that you asked me," she said. "I wanted to talk about it myself. We had two exceedingly narrow beds. He never let me buy anything except food. He alone was the buyer and he always looked for bargains. No, it wasn't good between us, and it reached a stage where I thanked God when he left me alone."

"What was he? Impotent?"

"Not exactly, but he did everything in dismal silence. I had often the impression I was having an affair with a corpse."

"No caresses?"

"In the beginning some, but later he cooled off completely. He was one of those old-fashioned men who believed that the purpose of marriage was only to have children. Since we couldn't have children, sexual relations were superfluous."

"Was he perverse in some sense?" I asked.

The woman thought it over. "In a sense, yes—you'll soon hear."

"What happened?" I asked.

"The worst trauma of our lives began with a joke."

"Whose joke?" I asked.

"Mine, not his. He was not a joker. Once in a while he tried to talk to me about stocks. God shouldn't punish me, but this topic bored me stiff. Later on I thought that I should have listened to him and shown some interest in his business, but somehow I couldn't do it. The moment he began to talk about it I started to yawn. I hated his business. A man should have a profession, do something, leave the house, not sit day and night and wait for stocks to go up or down a few cents. The fact is he didn't allow me to leave the house. He kept me prisoner. When I did go out to buy food I had to tell him in advance where I was going, what I was going to spend, and how long I'd be out of the house. I can't understand to this day how I could bear all this for five years. A war was going on, the Jews in Europe were destroyed, and I rationalized that my situation was still better than to languish in a concentration camp.

"One evening we were sitting together in our living room. I read the first pages of the newspaper, and he took out the business section. Suddenly he said, 'The oils are depressed.'

"I don't know why, but I said, 'So am I.'

"I'm not sure whether I said it to myself or to him. He looked at me, astonished, sad, angry, and asked, 'Why are you depressed? What do you miss? You aren't happy with me?'

"'It's only a joke,' I said.

"'Do you regret that you married me?' he asked. 'Do you want a divorce?'

"'No, Boris, I don't want a divorce,' I said.

"'Am I not the right husband for you?' he continued. 'Am I too old for you?'

"'And what if you are too old?' I asked. 'Can you become younger? Do you want to go to Professor Voronoff and implant monkey glands into your body?' I expected him to smile. I had heard there was a professor in Europe, I think in Switzerland, who tried to make the old young. I'm not sure Professor Voronoff was still alive at the time. I said it just to hear my own voice, perhaps to hear his voice. He looked at me not only with scorn but also with a kind of regret and pity. He said, 'I couldn't let you adopt a child, but if you want to adopt a young lover I have nothing against it.'

" 'Boris, I don't want to adopt anybody,' I said. 'It was just talk. It's time you weren't so literal, so serious.'

" 'Well, let it be so,' he said, and he left for the room he called his office.

"I think it was the winter of 1944. Hitler was on his way down, but the Jewish misfortune had no end. Reports came that all the Jews in Europe were doomed. I never heard Boris say anything about the Jewish situation. I lived all those years with a man I never understood and who remained a stranger to me.

"A few weeks passed, I don't remember how many. The last few days Boris had left the house before breakfast and did not return for lunch, as was his custom. This was something new in our lives. One evening he came home late. I waited for him in the living room and was reading a book I had borrowed from the public library. I had left his supper in the kitchen, but he told me he'd already eaten in a restaurant. He told me a son of his sister in London, a boy of fourteen, had come from England some time ago. His sister had feared that some misfortune would happen to him in the bombardments. The boy, whose name was Douglas, was a prodigy in mathematics and physics. He was accepted here in New York at a school for prodigies. Boris had consented that the boy should live with us. 'You never told me much about your sister,' I said. 'I had the impression you two were at odds.'

"'It's true,' he said, 'that we always disagreed. I was still a little boy when she married, to a man who was good for nothing, a perfect idiot, but her son, thank God, takes after my family, the Kozlovs. You'll not need to be alone any more. I want to tell you something else,' he continued. 'I've rented an office for myself. My business is expanding. I'm drowning in paperwork. I've begun to invest in stocks for some German refugees, and Brooklyn is too far for them. My office is in Manhattan.'

"Boris never spoke for so long, especially about his family. As a rule he only reproached me, and then he didn't speak, but screamed.

"I said to him, 'Everything comes so suddenly.'

"'Not so suddenly,' Boris said. 'I thought everything over very carefully.'

"'Why didn't you ever mention to me that your nephew is in America?' I asked.

"'I mention it now: He's an unusual boy. I took to him right away. He arrived here through Halifax, Nova Scotia. I'm sure you'll like him. He'll study in a special school for talented youngsters. Everything has already been arranged. Since my office is free now it can be his room. I'll buy him a bed, but until then he can sleep on the sofa. You have all the right to say no. I'm not going to force him on you.'

"'Boris, you know very well I'll agree,' I said.

"'He'll be here tomorrow morning,' Boris said, and went to his room.

"My first reaction when I heard the news was joy. I could not stand the loneliness anymore. God must have heard my prayers, I thought. But it soon became clear to me that Boris had contrived the whole plan in his conspiratorial manner. Men like Boris are bound by their nature to make plans way in advance and execute them precisely. They forget nothing. Even though he excoriated Stalin and called him a bloodthirsty Asian and a Genghis Khan of the twentieth century, I often thought Boris was a Stalin himself. We'll never know what people like these think. They always weave spider webs of vengeance. Did Boris bring this boy to tempt me and to be able later to sue me for infidelity? Was he connected with a lawyer? Was he in contact with another woman with a lot of money, or stocks? I could have easily saved him these sly tricks. If he had asked me for a divorce I would have given it to him without difficulties. I could still have gotten a job as a chambermaid or a saleswoman in a department store. During the war unemployment had ended. Nevertheless, I decided not to let myself be caught like an animal in a net. I intended to treat the boy from England with friendship but not to allow myself to fall into any entanglements.

"The next day Douglas came, and I'm ashamed to admit to you I fell in love with him at first sight. He was beautiful, slender, and tall for his age. Besides, he had a warmth that simply bewitched me. He called me 'Aunt,' but kissed me like a lover. He told me about his parents, and from his talk it became clear to me that his mother was a Boris in a skirt. She was a complete business-lady and had become rich from the war. She was separated from her husband, Douglas's father. The whole Kozlov family consisted of pedants and misanthropes, but Douglas seemed to have taken after his father, who came from a noble background. Douglas showed me his father's photograph. All my yearnings for a child and love, all my femininity and longings for motherhood had awakened in me. I kept reminding Douglas that he was still a child, that I could have been his mother, but he refused to listen to me.

"A day or two after Douglas's arrival Boris began to go to the office every morning, and I knew it was not accidental. There were times I wanted to ask Boris, 'What's the meaning of all this? What are you aiming at?' But I knew he would not tell me the truth. Together with the love for the boy I was assaulted by a silent fear of cold and cunning calculations. Someone had prepared a trap for me, and I was destined to fall into it."

"Did you fall into it?" I asked.

The old woman hesitated for a while. "Yes."

"Immediately?" I asked.

"Almost immediately," she said.

"How?"

"One night Boris did not come home to sleep. He had told me he was supposed to go to Boston, but I knew it was a lie. What did I have to lose? When a man goes to such lengths a woman has nothing to hope for. Boris did not come home, and Douglas without asking came into my bed. I never knew that a young boy like this could be so passionate."

"Those are supposed to be the man's strongest years." I said.

"Really? For me, it was partially curiosity and resignation. When someone spits on you you don't owe him any loyalty. Instead of spending one night in Boston Boris was gone three nights. I knew for sure he was in New York. Boston is not a center of stock speculation. When he finally called us and said that he was back in New York I told him, 'What you wanted did happen.'"

"What did he say?" I asked.

"He said that he did it all for me. I said, 'You didn't have to bring your nephew from England. You didn't have to go into such acrobatics,' but he kept on saying that he had seen that I was unhappy and he wanted to help me. I was afraid that he might try to punish Douglas. Who knows what goes on in such a crippled brain? However, when he came home that evening he was as friendly to the boy as before. He asked him many questions about school. We ate supper together, and I was surprised to see that Douglas did not show any embarrassment. Can a boy of his age be so clever and cynical? Did the two of them have an agreement? I still don't know the answer."

"How long did the whole thing last?" I asked.

"He came in the summer, and in the fall he was accepted to a college, not here in New York, but somewhere in the Middle West. He came to bid me farewell, and we spent the evening together. He told me that he would never forget me, that I'd enriched his life. He even promised he'd visit me on his winter vacation. He never smoked before, but that evening he smoked one cigarette after another. He brought me flowers and a bottle of cognac. I put the flowers into a vase and poured myself a tea glass of the drink, which I gulped down in the bathroom. He asked me about his uncle, and I told him that he would come home late, but I had to go to sleep early and that he must leave. 'Why,

Auntie?' he asked, and I said, 'Because I'm tired.' 'I hoped that we would spend the night together,' he said, and I said, 'The last night one has to spend with oneself.'

"He kissed me, and I told him to leave. He hesitated for a while, and then he left. I waited for a minute or two and then I jumped out the window. We lived on the fourth floor. Thank God, I fell on the pavement and not on an innocent passerby."

"You had made the decision earlier?" I asked.

"No, but I knew all the time that this was what Boris expected and I had to comply."

"Still, you remained alive and he did not succeed," I said.

"Yes, to my regret. This is the whole story. I once heard you say on the radio that you take many of your themes from readers who come to tell you their stories, and I decided to be one of them. All I ask is that you change the names."

"What does a person think in such seconds?" I asked.

"In such seconds one doesn't think: One does what fate wants you to."

"What happened since then?"

"Nothing really. I broke my arms. I broke my legs. I broke my skull, and the doctors tried to mend me. They are still trying."

"Where's Boris?"

"I never heard from him or his nephew. I believe they both are somewhere in England."

"You're not divorced?"

"What for? No. I get reparation monies from the Germans. I need little, but every few weeks I must go to the hospital. Thank God, they don't let me become a public charge. I won't live too much longer. I came to tell you only one thing: that of all the hopes a human being can have the most splendid is death. I tasted it, and whoever tasted this ecstasy must laugh at all the other so-called pleasures. That which man fears from the cradle to the grave is the highest joy."

"Still, seldom does anyone want to speed up this kind of joy," I said.

The woman did not answer and I thought she had not heard my words, but then she said, "The anticipation is part of the joy."

Translated by the author and
Lester Goran

THE POCKET
REMEMBERED

I n the Polish city of Plotzk there lived a man by the
name of Reb Amram Zalkind who was the court-Jew for
the squire, Count Bronislaw Walecki. The count was in no
way an enemy of the Jews; he traded with them and often
consulted them in business. It was the custom among the
Polish squires that when they gave a ball, the court-Jew
made the guests merry. He disguised himself as a bear,
growled, and crawled on all fours, and the guests had something to laugh at and to mock. But the squire Walecki
looked down upon this barbaric custom. He sat Reb Amram
among the other guests when he gave a ball and had the
cook prepare vegetables in a special pot to assure the Jew
that the food was kosher. The squire owned many forests
in which the trees were logged and floated on rafts down
the Vistula to Danzig, where German merchants bought
the lumber. Reb Amram spoke Polish and German well,
and the squire frequently sent him to fairs in Danzig and
Leipzig. He bought all kinds of jewelry there; rings, chains,
bracelets, brooches, earrings, and various precious stones
for the squires, for the Countess Helena Walecki, and for
her daughters. Reb Amram was not a learned man, but he

remembered the law that if you owe but one groschen, even to someone overseas, you must go there and repay the debt, since only the sins committed against God, not against man, are forgiven on Yom Kippur. Reb Amram could have easily become rich the way many dishonest stewards, marshalls, and usurers did, but he was by nature an honest man. In handling the squire's money, he accounted for every groschen. Even Reb Amram's enemies acknowledged that in money matters he was upright. In those times, traveling salesmen wrote everything down on a small chalkboard, but Reb Amram had purchased a pen and a notebook to keep records of his accounts. His coat had two deep pockets, one for expenditures and another for income. All his personal earnings he kept in a separate leather purse. At every opportunity the squire Walecki praised his court-Jew and his honesty.

In time Reb Amram became quite wealthy. Envious townspeople gossiped behind his back and hinted that he only feigned honesty but was actually cheating the squire. They maintained that a Jew who works so closely with a squire could not avoid drinking non-kosher wine or looking and lusting after the female gentry because Alte Trina, Amram's wife, was as small as a midget and slightly hunchbacked. Reb Amram was tall and straight, with blue eyes and a blonde beard. Only a few white hairs could be seen on his head and beard, even though he was approaching sixty. He had a strong singing voice and was the leader of the morning prayer on the High Holidays and also the blower of the *shofar*. The young matrons in the women's section of the synagogue savored his voice. Their mothers-in-law used to reproach: them "Look into the prayer book, not at Amram."

As small and as frail as Alte Trina was, she bore Amram four sons and three daughters, and they all married well. It seemed that affluence was Reb Amram's lot. He did not, God forbid, say: "It was the might of my own hands that brought me this great wealth." He often contributed to charity. On Sabbath or on a holiday he never returned from the synagogue without a poor guest. He gave generously to the society which married off orphaned maidens, to the watchers of the sick, toward purchasing sacred books for the study house, and for redeeming innocent prisoners. Alte Trina sent chicken soup to the sick in the poorhouse.

One summer a fair took place in Leipzig. Reb Amram Zalkind was sent there to meet with foreign merchants, to claim the debts which they owed the squire and to negotiate down payments for new orders. The squire Walecki was marrying off his youngest daughter, the Countess Marianna, to the son of Count Zamoyski, one of the richest noblemen in Poland, and the squiress asked Reb Amram to buy for the bride-to-be a strand of pearls, a variety of gold utensils, as well as silk, velvet, fine linen, and various other costly materials. Reb Amram carefully wrote every item down in his notebook. He would be handling large sums of money, and he made sure that every purchase was recorded clearly, and no mistake, God forbid, should be made in the account. He told Alte Trina not to worry about him and not to expect him back too early, since business trips like these took much time. He said to her, "With God's help I will be back for the High Holidays."

Outside, Merkel, his coachman, was waiting in a *britska* harnessed with two horses. Because he traveled so often, Reb Amram knew the prayer before embarking on a journey by heart. Reishe, the maid, brought him a basket of food, and Reb Amram rode off onto the highway which crossed the Prussian border into Leipzig. The journey was not without danger. Robbers as well as wild animals lurked on the highways. The Poles and the Prussians constantly waged wars and minor battles. The customs officials harassed the traveling merchants, especially the Jews who carried no swords and could not defend themselves. But, thank God, there was no mishap on this trip. They knew Reb Amram in the inns and prepared comfortable lodgings for him with strictly kosher meals. He always kept loose change—gratuities for the servants. Reb Amram had often visited Leipzig, but the city was never as full as this time. Traders had come not only from Germany and Poland but also from Russia, Italy, France—even from Spain, Portugal, and England. The inns were packed; foreign languages were heard. People could barely push their way through in the marketplace filled with covered wagons, carts, and carriages. Commodities were displayed which Reb Amram had never seen before. He was surrounded with lumber dealers and those who imported grain, flax, and hides from Poland. In addition to all the commotion a traveling circus had come to town with bears, lions, elephants, and horses which were trained to dance to the sound of music. Despite high taxes and vicious decrees imposed upon them, the Jews engaged in many trades and had almost all the banks at their disposal. With letters of credit written in Hebrew or in Yiddish they could borrow all the money they needed.

The majority of Jewish bankers kept their capital in their pockets or in hollow belts they strapped around their waists. The Jewish merchants lodged and ate together. Generally the Gentile tradesmen got drunk toward evening, sang wild songs, and danced in the taverns with women. Leipzig attracted shady females who entertained the men. Prostitutes from all over came to the fairs. Although Reb Amram was a pious Jew, a man of the Torah, he somewhat envied the libertines who indulged in all their passions. Alte Trina was always weak. Even in her clean days she had often dismissed him with various excuses; a headache, a toothache, a burning at the pit of the stomach, a chill in the bones. In her older years she became a broken shard. Reb Amram had entirely secluded himself from her because no matter how he approached her, she immediately began to cry that he was hurting her. The evil spirit which lurks in each man and waits for him to become greedy for the pleasures of the flesh often chided Reb Amram:

"Amram, you suffer needlessly. You wait for rewards in the world to come, but it doesn't exist. What people don't grab for themselves in this world is lost forever. For almost two thousand years the Jews have anticipated the coming of their Messiah and He has still not arrived. They will go on waiting until the year six thousand. There is no Paradise, no Hell. The righteous do not feed on Leviathan, they don't drink the holy wine stored up for the saints, they don't wear crowns on their heads or enjoy the radiance of the Shechinah. They rot in their graves and are devoured by worms. The sinners are clever. As long as they can they live it up."

The evil spirit exhibited erudition: "If there was a hereafter, why is it not mentioned in the Bible? On the contrary, it is written in the Book of Ecclesiastes: 'And the dead know not anything.' Even one of the Amorites denied the coming of the Messiah. Our ancient patriarchs, even Moses, were lecherous. Judah, whose name all Jews carry, went to a harlot."

Night fell. There was such a crush of people in the streets that Reb Amram could barely squeeze his way through. Music shrieked from taverns. The sounds of fiddles, trumpets, whistles could be heard as drummers drummed, hands clapped, feet stamped. The shouting of drunken males was mixed with salacious female laughter. From the open doors rose a heat like from an oven and odors of wines, liquors, mead, beer, as well as of roasted chickens, geese, lamb, pork, all kinds of herbs and spices. Reb Amram had eaten a large dinner: chopped liver with onions, tripe, calves' feet, noodles with gravy, beef and horseradish, and later compote with plums and apricots. Nevertheless, the non-kosher smells aroused a fresh appetite and a thirst in him. He sensed a mighty strength in his limbs. He felt he could wrench a tree out of the earth with all its roots. When he passed an iron street lamp, a boyish need arose in him to show off and try to bend it. As he stood there contemplating his own prowess, a small woman with fiery red hair came over to him. She had green eyes like a cat, a round face, cheeks caked with rouge. She wore a short yellow dress and green high-heeled boots with black stockings. She gave him a sweet smile, revealing a full mouth of small teeth, and asked with a young voice, "Where are you from, buddy? From Poland?"

Reb Amram became so confused by her presence that for

a moment he lost his tongue. Many whores had stopped him on his way, but they all spoke German, not Yiddish. He had heard that there were also Jewish whores in the big cities, but he had never encountered any. After a while he came to himself and answered: "Yes, from Poland."

"I am also from Poland," the woman said. "But I've been away for a long time."

"From where in Poland?" Reb Amram asked.

"From Piask."

"From the Piask thieves?" Reb Amram asked, and soon regretted his words. He feared she might curse him or spit at him. It was not in his nature to insult anyone. How do they say it? As long as a word is in the mouth, the mouth is the ruler; when it leaves the mouth, the word is the ruler. Thank God, the woman did not become enraged but answered him good-naturedly: "Not all Chelmites are fools and not all Piaskers are thieves. There are honest people in Piask too."

"Forgive me, I was only joking," Reb Amram apologized.

"The truth is that there were a lot of thieves in Piask, but my father was an honest man, a tailor."

"How did you end up here?" Reb Amram asked.

The woman paused and said, "It's a long story. I fell in love with a bear trainer—actually, not as much with him as with the bear. I was barely twelve years old but I was already yearning to sow my wild oats. Both the bear trainer and the bear died a long time ago, but since then I have been dragging around with this circus. They pay me water on kasha so I have to earn a few extra gulden after the performance. The other women do it too."

"Do you have a room here?" Reb Amram asked.

"I rent one for a few hours. Come."

She started to go, and Amram followed her with hesitation. He heard the evil spirit say, "There is no God, there is none. Even if there were a God, he would not remember every sin in every city at every fair in every land from India to Ethiopia. This whole game of piety is not worth a sniff of tobacco."

The woman led Reb Amram into a dark alley, to a structure which looked like a stable, and she opened a door. A wick was burning in a shard with oil. A straw mat was spread on the floor.

"This is it?" Reb Amram asked.

"Yes. Two guldens!" Saying these words, the strumpet extended one hand for the money and with the other hand she opened her blouse quickly and displayed two stiff breasts with fiery red nipples. With one yank she tore open the buttons of her skirt and remained stark naked except for her shoes and gartered stockings. She did something like a somersault on the straw mat. "Come!" Reb Amram was about to throw himself on her, but at that moment he heard a terrible cry, "You are losing the world to come."

Reb Amram shuddered. He recognized the voice of his father, who had died more than twenty years before. Reb Amram started running, and he beat his head against the door. He almost tripped over the threshold. The woman screamed as if possessed, but Reb Amram ran through the darkness in a state of confusion and fear as if he were chased by murderers. The alley was full of potholes, stones, and unharnessed wagons. He crashed into the pole of a wagon, immediately receiving a bump on his forehead. His knee was scraped. He didn't know whether he was fleeing toward the residential area of Leipzig or to the outskirts of the city. He raised his eyes, and the sky was seeded with myriad stars. One star tore away from its constellation and swept over the sky, leaving behind a luminous trace. The heavens seemed ablaze with a divine conflagration.

As Reb Amram was running he remembered the commentary of Gemara on the Joseph story in the Book of Genesis: When Potiphar's wife grabbed Joseph by the sleeve and requested that he lie with her, Joseph was ready to fall into depravity, but his father's image revealed itself to him and helped him resist the temptation. "The dead live!" a voice screamed into Reb Amram's ears or into his mind. "There is Special Providence. They see everything on High, every move a man is about to make; they read his mind, they weigh his deeds, they watch his steps."

Dogs barked at Reb Amram, tried to bite him, but he pushed them away with his boots, murmuring the words from the Pentateuch: "But against any of the children of Israel not even a dog will whet its tongue." Although he knew it was dangerous he ran through the forest where thieves and highwaymen loitered. They could have killed him there and no rooster would have crowed. He was escaping from a harlot, a demon, followed by the Angel of Death. His feet became strangely light. He skipped over fallen trees, puddles, heaps of garbage. The sweat ran over his face, cramps gnawed at his stomach, and he regurgitated a nauseating sour-sweet fluid. His belly blew up hard like a drum. In his distress it occurred to him that for the first time in his life he had forgotten to recite the afternoon prayer. He spoke aloud to the sacred soul of his deceased father, thanking him for guarding him against the pitfall of lechery. He asked his father's spirit to protect him from robbers, since he was carrying the squire's money and if he returned with empty hands, they would suspect him of theft.

Thank God he managed to return to the city of Leipzig. Only now did he feel the pain in his forehead and in his knee. One of the dogs had bitten into his leg and its teeth had torn through his pants. Reb Amram knew he was saved from many perils, those of the soul and of the body. He would have to recite the prayer for escaping danger twice and to redeem himself through much charity and many virtuous deeds. He arrived at the guest-house where he was staying. The entrance was dark, but he heard talking and laughter from the kitchen and the chambers upstairs. What should he tell the owner of the guest-house, the guests, his own coachman? They would see that something bad had happened to him and query him. He was limping, his face was swollen, his boots were covered with horse dung and mud. He had to quickly think up a lie. Reb Amram recalled the saying from *The Ethics of the Fathers*: "One sin drags another sin after it." He stood in the darkness frightened by what had happened to him, baffled by his miraculous rescue, disgraced by his evil passions. He didn't dare to utter the name of the Lord with his defiled lips. He wasn't crying, but his eyes were burning and his cheeks were hot. He was on the verge of utter degradation and the fires of Gehenna.

Thank God the trip back to Poland went through without any mishap. Reb Amram brought back everything which the squire and squiress had ordered, along with lumber contracts and a considerable amount of down payments. He had written down every groschen he had spent in his book. After the squire and the squiress thanked Reb Amram profusely for his diligence and good judgment in business, the squire and Reb Amram went into a separate room. Taking out heaps of golden ducats from his belt and various pockets, Reb Amram began to count the money. He had kept the bank notes and contracts in an oaken box with brass fasteners and a steel lock. As always, he hoped the accounts would balance out to the last penny. But strangely, five golden ducats were missing from one account. "How is this possible?" Reb Amram asked himself. The squire, who trusted Reb Amram implicitly, dismissed the matter with a wave of the hand. He insisted that Reb Amram surely forgot to write down some small expense. When he remembered it, the account would straighten itself out. Reb Amram offered to give the squire the missing ducats from his own purse, but the squire refused to hear of it. He argued, "It doesn't pay to be so concerned over such a petty sum." The squire was familiar not only with the New Testament but also with the Old Testament, and he quoted the words Ephron said to Abraham when he bought the Cave of Machpaleh from him: "What are four hundred silver shekels between you and me?"

Reb Amram promised not to worry about it, but when he went back home his spirit remained troubled, partly from the ordeal with the lewd female and partly because of the lost ducats. He sat up half the night and made calculations.

He remembered every groschen he spent in Leipzig, even the alms which he had distributed among the beggars in the marketplace. But these five ducats seemed to have slipped between his fingers. Had somebody robbed him? Did this Piask trollop steal them? He was sure she had not stood so close to him that she could put her hand into his pocket. While pondering the lost ducats he realized he forgot to bring his wife, Alte Trina, a gift, as he always did when he returned from a journey. She had not mentioned a word about it, but he imagined that she greeted him less warmly than usual when he came home. He had also neglected to bring a gift for the maid.

Reb Amram awoke in the middle of the night and lay awake until daybreak. While undressing, he had discovered a knot in the sash of his pants. He often made such a knot as a reminder to pay a bill, to answer a letter, or to give money to a needy charity. Now it had slipped his mind when and for what reason he had made this particular sign. He fell asleep at dawn, and the Piask woman came to him in a dream. She stood before him naked, her red hair loose, and she was singing a song which he had once heard in a tavern:

Oy vey give me tea
Tea is bitter
Give me sugar
Sugar is sweet
Give me feet
Feet are wet
Come in bed
In bed no sheet

Come in street
The street is dark
Come in park
In park no light
Hold me tight
In mud and mire
Burn like fire

Reb Amram awoke with a start and with passion. The
month of Elul was approaching, but he was wallowing in
lewd fantasies. "Woe is me, I am sunk in iniquities" he
mumbled. Normally Reb Amram waited impatiently for
the Days of Awe to recite the morning prayers at the pulpit
in the synagogue, dressed for the occasion in a white robe
and a gold embossed miter. Weeks before he usually went
over the tunes and the liturgies and practiced the *shofar*
which he would blow. But now Reb Amram no longer
yearned to lead the community in prayer. None other than
Poorah, the Angel of Forgetfulness, must have accompanied him that fateful evening when he had encountered the
harlot in Leipzig. He could not even remember the explanation he offered the people at the inn for the bump on his
forehead and for his torn trousers and filthy boots. And
what should he tell the squire about the missing five ducats?
Although Reb Amram was prepared to repay him from his
own money, the danger of being disgraced was far from
over. It was possible that the coachman had already relayed
the strange event to the squire. Gossip travels quickly. Reb
Amram did not want to contradict himself and be labeled
a liar.

He fell asleep and immediately the red-haired female appeared anew. He saw her descend the stairs of the Plotzk ritual bathhouse. She immersed herself three times, and her hair spread over the water like a red web. She began to climb out, winking at Reb Amram. "What happened?" Reb Amram asked himself. "Have I married her and she is taking her ablutions? Is she cleansing herself for my sake? And where is Alte Trina? Is she, God forbid, no longer among the living?" He shuddered and awoke. "This female is one of Lilith's demons whom she sends at night to seduce God-fearing men to pollution," Reb Amram said to himself. "I must not lead the congregation in prayer any longer. The prayers from one such as I will not reach up to Heaven. They might even, perish the thought, bring evil decrees on the town—pestilence, famine, bloodshed." Reb Amram felt compelled to give the trustees of the synagogue advance notice to find a replacement.

As in the Book of Job, one evil tiding followed another. That morning, after Reb Amram woke up from his troubled sleep, even before he went to pray, he heard the sound of a horseman approaching his house. It was a messenger informing Reb Amram that the squire had sent for him. Reb Amram was shaken up. Who knows? Maybe the coachman saw him with the wanton female and reported it to the squire. Even though the squire was himself guilty of adultery, he probably expected the right conduct from his subordinates. "*Nu*, my seven good years are over," Reb Amram murmured to himself. He let the *britska* be harnessed and went to the squire. Thank God, the squire received him in a friendly way. Reb Amram began to speak about the vanished gold ducats, but the squire interrupted him:

"Don't be foolish, Amram, what are five ducats to me?

I trust my entire estate to you and you make a fuss over a pittance. If it would have been a matter of a thousand ducats I would not worry. I have sent for you because I have to ask you a favor."

"The squire wants a favor from me?" Reb Amram asked in astonishment.

"Yes. A big favor. I find it distasteful to request this of you, but I have no choice. A few days ago I met with my future in-laws, the Count Zamoyski and his wife, the Countess. You certainly know how influential they are in Poland and what a great honor it is for my wife and myself to marry off our beloved daughter to their son. The Countess stems from even a higher lineage than her husband. She is a descendant of a king in Poland. As you know we are preparing for a wedding which will not be equaled in the history of Poland. The Count told me that his court-Jew, Reb Nissel, who is learned in the Bible and in the Talmud and is an experienced merchant to boot, is also a talented actor. Whenever the Zamoyskis give a ball, Reb Nissel disguises himself as a bear and amuses the guests. I had told him about you and I praised you to Heaven. The Count mentioned in passing, 'If your Amram is as clever and as witty as my Nissel, why don't they perform together at the wedding of our children and entertain us?' I tried to explain to the Count that you are of a different breed, that it is beneath your dignity to act as a comedian. I told him that I have never requested a service like this from you. But the Count became adamant about the idea. He literally demanded it from me to have you perform with his court-Jew. This is how the Zamoyskis are: strong-willed and adventurous. They always could have anything under the sun. No one has ever refused them anything. I will make it short. I was practically forced to promise the Count that I would ask you to consent. I assure you that this will be the first and last time. I have persuaded the Count to agree that Reb Nissel will perform the role of the bear and you will be the bear trainer. You can lead Reb Nissel by a rope and converse intermittently. All the high-class guests will admire your facetious dialogue. I know that you are familiar with Jewish humor and wit. It is not such a shame to play the role of a bear trainer. I promise you that if you will ever need a favor from me, no matter how great, I will do it for you with pleasure."

As the squire spoke, Reb Amram felt as if a fist clutched at his heart and crushed it with a mighty force. Reb Amram had heard that court-Jews performed at squires' balls and made the guests merry, but he never wanted to stoop to that level. Reb Amram knew that this request of the squire was a punishment from heaven for dallying with the red-headed whore even for a few minutes. He felt like crying out: "Your Excellency, everything yes, but this is too much of a blow." Instead he asked, "When will the wedding take place?"

The squire told him the date. Reb Amram quickly figured out that the wedding was to fall on the first day of Succot. While other Jews would be sitting in the *succot* under the wings of the Shechinah being hosts to the souls of such saints as Abraham, Isaac, and Jacob; Aaron, Moses, and David; he, Amram, would be leading another Jew, dressed up like a bear, by a rope, and make a mockery of himself and of the scholarly Reb Nissel before a band of murderers and pagans. Because what are all squires in essence? How did they manage to rule the land if not by the power of the sword? How did they reduce all the peasants to slaves and force the people of Israel, whom God has chosen above all other nations, to become their underlings?

"What is your answer?" the squire asked with a trace of impatience.

"If I will be able to, I will do it" Reb Amram answered.

"Why should you not be able to?"

"Everything is in God's hands."

For a while they were both silent. Afterwards, the squire said, "I understand very well how difficult this task is for you in your age and in your position. But I am afraid of opposing this powerful family. Today they are my friends, tomorrow my bloody enemies."

"Yes, true."

"You seem tired, Reb Amram. Go home and rest up."

"Yes, I will do so. Thank you, Your Excellency."

"Why does God allow people to tyrannize one another? What does your Talmud say about this?" the squire asked.

Reb Amram thought it over. "Everything is created so that people can choose between good and evil."

"Not always," and the squire made a gesture which meant that the audience was over.

Returning home, Reb Amram saw Alte Trina sitting on the bench in front of the house knitting a sock. He was surprised, since she seldom sat on the bench outside at this time of the day but was usually busy in the kitchen preparing a meal. He looked at her for a while. They already had grandchildren together, but it seemed to him that only yesterday they were still young. In those years he could barely wait for her to go to the ritual bath so that he could approach her. Now she was an old woman, her face withered and wrinkled. A few white hairs had sprouted under her chin, a little female beard. With the knitting needle she scratched her earlobe, which protruded from her bonnet, and asked, "What did the squire want from you? Why did he send for you so early in the morning? I worried myself sick over your safety."

"Nothing, Alte Trina. It had to do with his daughter's wedding."

"What does he want now?"

"Oh, something about the jewelry which I had bought for her."

"How many trinkets do they need? She will be bedecked with gold and diamonds from head to toe. They forget, the fools, that people don't live forever." Alte Trina changed her tone. "You look pale, Amram. This trip has exhausted you."

"No danger."

"Why did you run there so early? You hadn't even prayed."

"If the squire sends a courier, you can't keep him waiting."

"I will give you a glass of milk. This, one is allowed to drink before praying."

"No, Alte Trina. Let me first put on my prayer shawl and phylacteries."

"Amram, wait, I must have a word with you."

"What do you want?"

Alte Trina brought over a chair and made Reb Amram sit down. "Amram, maybe I shouldn't say this, but you are traveling down a crooked path. If a stranger would say this you might suspect him of being your enemy, but I am your wife, the mother of your children, and I only want the best for you. Believe me, if someone would ask me to lay down my head for your sake I would gladly do it."

"Speak clearly. What am I doing which is crooked?"

"First of all, you work too hard. A man of your age—you should live to be a hundred and twenty—doesn't need to drag himself off to fairs in distant lands. You know very well that the roads are teeming with thieves and assassins. Does it pay to risk one's health so that some *shikse* can dangle her jewelry before an impudent idolator? Recently I heard that Count Zamoyski was hunting during the harvest season along with a band of noblemen. Their horses and dogs trampled and ruined hundreds of acres of fields ready for the harvest, and when the peasants pleaded with the villains not to turn God's blessings into a shambles and bring famine to the villages, they fell into such a rage that they shot with their pistols and killed a number of them. Imagine, Amram, it is their peasants, their estates, but these drunkards think they are entitled to do anything they please. People have told me that the young Count had set fire to stacks of wheat which had been prepared for the thrashers. Your squire is planning for a wedding which will cost him a fortune. He is already in debt over his head. The end will be that he will go broke. And when they get into trouble they come to borrow from the Jew. Then if you don't give to them willingly, they take by force."

"For the time being, our squire is not to blame." Reb Amram said.

"So you believe," Alte Trina went on. "There is a second thing I have to say to you. You had told me that, God willing, after we married off our youngest child that we would put all business aside and devote ourselves only to Jewishness. You even mentioned going to the Holy Land."

"To the Holy Land? Old people go there, not people of our age. I don't remember saying this."

"You don't remember, but I do. And God certainly remembers."

Reb Amram had a desire to scold her as always when she interfered too much in his affairs, but he recalled the squire's humiliating proposal to him and restrained himself. He shrugged, "Alte Trina, we'll talk about this later."

"Again later?"

"Let me finish the prayers first."

Reb Amram entered the room where he kept his bookcases and prepared himself for prayer. He put on the prayer shawl, the phylacteries, wound the throngs around his arm, and began to murmur the appropriate prayers. But he was distracted by confusing thoughts, and he prayed without concentration. He even overlooked certain verses. To become a buffoon for the squire's sake? Lead Reb Nissel by a rope and crack jokes? Reb Amram stood up to recite the eighteen benedictions, but he omitted some passages and others he repeated. He resorted to addressing God in Yiddish, "Father in Heaven, I am in a terrible predicament. Save me or take me away."

Reb Amram then realized that prayer of this nature is a sin. A human being has no right to dictate to the Almighty or to admonish Him. After a while he took off the prayer shawl and the phylacteries. A strong fatigue had come over him, and he felt a weakness in his knees. He locked the door which led to the corridor, collapsed onto the sofa, and fell into a deep sleep. As if the Lord of dreams could scarcely wait for Reb Amram to fall asleep, He immediately brought him to Leipzig. It was again night and he was standing with the red-headed harlot by a lamppost. Again, the Evil One cajoled him to damnation. This time Reb Amram saw Satan's fiendish image: taller than the lamppost, dark and sheer as a spider web, with horns like a he-goat, two holes instead of eyes, and the mouth of a frog. He whispered to Reb Amram, "Take her, the whore. Go into her. Have no fear. There is no law below, there is no judge above. And even if there would be a God somewhere in the Seventh Heaven, He would not remember all the petty prohibitions, all the silly restrictions and interpretations from the time of Moses until the time of some half-witted rabbi in a muddy village."

In his dream, Reb Amram followed the harlot and she led him into the dark hallway and opened the door of the murky shed. A wick burned in the shard with oil; a straw mat lay on the floor. In a sweep the whore threw down the colorful rags and called out: "Two guldens. Come!" Reb Amram again heard his father's cry: "You're losing the world to come!" He started to run and as he ran, he pushed his hand into his pocket and threw a handful of gold coins to the raging harlot. Reb Amram woke up instantly. The hand which threw the coins was still shaking, and his feet were scampering as if running. For a moment Reb Amram took the dream for reality. He was both in the study where he had prayed and in the shed with the whore. He fell on the floor, his teeth chattering. He lingered a while until he could fully grasp where he was. Despite all his anxiety Reb Amram realized that the dream had solved his riddle. In his consternation he had thrown the fee of the harlot from the pocket where he kept the squire's money. He had forgotten this but the pocket, a piece of fabric and lining, remembered and computed the balance accordingly—a silent witness that may testify against him on the Day of Judgment.

Reb Amram felt like laughing and crying. If a pocket is able to remember, what about the Almighty, of Whom it is said: "There is no forgetfulness before Thy Throne of Glory."

"Merciful God, have pity on me." Reb Amram called out. "My father in Paradise, you are not dead, you live. Your sacred soul protected me in Leipzig. You hovered over me, kept a vigil during the entire journey, guarded my every step and did not allow me to fall into the net of debauchery, to sink to the lowest abyss. There is a God, there is. There is a hereafter, there is," Reb Amram shouted in his mind to Satan the spoiler. "How could I have forgotten all this and let myself go with a prostitute, about whom King Solomon says, 'None that go unto her return again, neither take they hold of the paths of life.' God sees and the saints see and there is no death, there is none!"

Somebody knocked at the door—Alte Trina. How strange, but the moment he saw her he also recalled the meaning of the knot in his sash: to buy for her the new edition of *Tsennah Urennah*, the Yiddish translation of the Pentateuch and its commentaries, since the binding of her old volume was torn and some pages had fallen out.

That day Reb Amram sent back the five gold coins to the squire by messenger. Later, he told the elders of the community that he was sick in his stomach and must see a doctor in Warsaw. In case, God forbid, he doesn't recover, they would have to find another leader for the morning prayers on the High Holidays and another man to blow the *shofar*. He harnessed the *britska* himself, took Alte Trina with him, and left only Reishe the maid at home. He gave her a large sum of money to cover all her expenses in case of a long absence.

Reb Amram did not come back for the High Holidays. He never returned to Plotzk. After some time his sons and daughters came to town and brought a letter from their father saying that he was giving up his house and the books for preachers and Talmudic scholars who came to the city. Reb Amram's sons and daughters brought additional money for Merkel the coachman and for Reishe the maid as well as a letter signed by Alte Trina which transferred ownership of her clothing and utensils to Reishe.

The wedding of Count Zamoyski's son and Walecki's daughter never came to pass. A few days before the wedding the young count went hunting in the forest and one of the hunters mistook him for an animal and shot him dead. Walecki's daughter, the bride, fell into a melancholia from this dismal event and she decided to enter a cloister.

Nobody heard from Reb Amram for over two years. Some believed that he was still visiting important doctors and healers in far-off cities. Others concluded that Reb Amram and his wife were no longer among the living. One day a rabbinical messenger from Jerusalem arrived in Plotzk and brought a letter from Reb Amram. Reb Amram wrote that after many months of wanderings and tribulations he and his wife miraculously managed to arrive by ship in the Land of Israel. In Jerusalem they found a place to live. From the money which he saved and which Alte Trina had received from selling her jewelry, they now could afford to

devote their old years to Jewishness. He studies the Mishnah in the study house of Rabbi Yehuda the Chassid and
recites Psalms at the Wailing Wall in the corner where the
Shechinah has always been present. In the month of Elul he
and Alte Trina visit the graves of Mother Rachel, Rabbi
Simon ben Yochai, and other saints. They have traveled to
the city of Safad, and he has immersed himself in the ritual
bath of the holy Isaac Luria. The sky in the Land of Israel
is higher than in other countries, the stars are brighter, and
the air is as clear as crystal and as sweet as wine. Reb
Amram requested that the townspeople of Plotzk help the
messenger collect money for a yeshiva because in Heaven
are kept records of every groschen a man contributes to
charity or, God forbid, to means of transgression. He ended
the letter with the puzzling words: "A man forgets, but
his pocket remembers."

Translated by Deborah Menashe

THE SMUGGLER

The telephone rang, and when I answered I heard a murmuring, a stuttering and coughing. After a while a man said, "You most probably forgot about it, but you once promised to inscribe my books, I mean your books. In Philadelphia where we met you gave me your address and telephone number. Your address is the same but you've changed your telephone to a private number. I got it from your secretary but I had to promise her that I wouldn't take much of your time."

He tried to remind me of my speech that evening in Philadelphia and I realized it had happened some ten years ago. He said to me, "Are you hiding? In those days one could still find you in the telephone book. I do the same thing in my own small way. I avoid people."

"Why?" I asked.

"To explain this would take too much time and I promised not to bother you too long."

We made an appointment. He was supposed to come to my apartment late in the evening. It was in December and a heavy snow had fallen in New York. From his idiomatic Yiddish it was clear to me he must be one of those Polish refugees who emigrated to America long after the war. Those who came to America in the earlier years interspersed their Yiddish with English words. I stood at the window and looked out on Broadway. The street below was white and the sky had a violet tinge. The radiator was seething quietly and sang out a tune which reminded me of our tiled stove on Krochmalna Street and the cricket behind it and the kerosene lamp over my father's desk. From experience I knew that those who make appointments with me come earlier than the agreed time. I expected any moment to hear a ringing at the door, but half an hour passed and he did not show up. I was looking for stars in the reddish sky, but I knew in advance that I would not find one in the New York heavens. Then I heard something like a scratch at my door. I went to open it and I saw a little man behind a pushcart heaped up with books. In the cold winter my guest wore a shabby raincoat and a shirt with an open collar and a knitted cap on his head. He asked, "Your door has no bell?"

"Here's the bell button," I said.

"What? I'm half blind. It all comes with the years. We don't die at once but on the installment plan."

"Where did you get so many books of mine? Well, come in."

"I don't want to make your rug wet. I will leave the cart outside. No one will steal it."

"It doesn't matter. Come in."

I helped the man push the cart into the corridor. "I didn't know I'd brought out so many books," I said, and then I asked, "Have I really written so many books in my life?"

"They're not all yours. I also have books about you here,

and various magazines and journals as well as translations."

After a while we went into the living room, and I said, "It's winter outside and you're dressed as if it were summer. Aren't you cold?"

"Cold, no. My father, he should rest in peace, used to say, 'No one wears a mask to cover one's nose. The nose doesn't get cold. A poor man is all made of nose flesh.'"

He smiled, and I saw that he had no teeth. I asked him to sit down. He looked to me like those men who live out of doors, like one of those beggars and bums one sees on the Bowery and in the hotels for the homeless. But I also saw the gentleness of his narrow face and in his eyes.

"Where do you keep all these books?" I asked. "In your apartment where you live?"

He shrugged his shoulders. "I live nowhere," he said. "In our little village in Poland there were yeshiva boys who ate every day in a different home. I sleep every night in a different house. I have here a brother-in-law, the husband of my late sister, and I sleep in his house two nights a week. I have a friend, a landsman, and I can sleep over there when there's a need. I used to live in a building in Williamsburg in Brooklyn, but the house was condemned and they wrecked it. While I was sick in the hospital thieves stole everything except my books. My landsman keeps them in his basement. I get reparation money from the Germans. After what happened to my family and my people I don't want to be settled anyplace."

"What did you do before the war?" I asked.

The man pondered for a while and smiled. "I did what you told me to do in one of your articles, to smuggle myself, to sneak by, to muddle through. I was reading you in Poland. You once wrote that human nature is such that one cannot do anything in a straight line. You always have to maneuver between the powers of wickedness and madness.

"In the time of the first World War, I was still a little boy, but my mother and sister smuggled meat from Galicia and brought back from there tobacco and other contraband. Without this we would have all starved to death. When they were caught they were beaten cruelly. There were five children in our home, an old grandmother, a cripple, and my father, who could do nothing except study Mishnah and recite psalms or the Zohar. I asked him why all these plagues descended on us and he said the same thing you said. In exile one cannot live normally. One must always steal one's way among those who have the power and carry weapons. The moment a man gets some power he becomes wicked, my father said. The one who keeps a knife stabs, the one who has a gun shoots, and the one who has a pen writes laws which are always on the side of the thieves and murderers. When I became older and I began to read worldly books I convinced myself that what my father said about the Jewish people was true about the whole human race and even about the animals. The wolves devour the sheep, the lions kill the zebras. In later years we had in our village communists who said that Comrades Lenin and Stalin would bring justice, but it soon became clear that they behaved like all the others who had power in all generations. Today a victim, tomorrow a tyrant. I read about Darwin and Malthus. These were the laws of life and I decided my father was right. After Poland became independent smuggling ceased, but as always might was right. I hadn't learned any trade, and even if I'd learned how to be a tailor or a shoemaker I hadn't the slightest desire to sit ten hours a day and sew buttons or tack heels and soles on boots. I certainly did not have the desire to get married and create new victims for the new killers. Two of my younger brothers had become communists and ended up in Stalin's prisons or the gold mines of the north. A third brother went to Israel and fell from an Arab bullet. My parents and a sister died by the Nazis. Yes, I became a smuggler, and what I smuggled was myself. My body is my contraband. My coming here to America in 1949 was, I may say, a triumph of my smuggling. The chances for me to remain alive and come to the United States were smaller than small. If you ask me what my occupation is my answer is, 'I am a Yiddish poet.' How can you know whether a person is a poet or not? If an editor needs to fill a hole in his magazine and he publishes a poem of yours, then you are a poet. If it doesn't happen then you're just a graphomaniac. I never had any luck with editors and so I belong to the second category."

"May I ask why you need autographs?" I said.

"Some little madness everyone must have. If Jack the Ripper were resurrected from his grave people would run to get his autograph, especially women. I was given an ego, a wanter, and I wage war with it. It wants to eat but I tell it to fast. It wants honors but I bring shame on it. Ego-schmego, I call it, hunger-schmunger. I do everything to spite it. It wants fresh rolls for breakfast and I give it stale bread. It likes strong coffee but I make it drink tepid water from the faucet. It still dreams about young women but it remains a virgin. Ten times a day I tell it, 'Get away from me, I need you like a hole in the head; you play the part of a friend but you're my worst enemy.' Just for spite I make it read old newspapers which I find on the floor of the subway. Thank God, I'm the stronger one, at least strong enough to make it miserable."

"Do you believe in God?" I asked.

"Yes, I do. The scientists tell us that a cosmic bomb exploded twenty billion years ago and it created all the worlds. A week does not pass when they don't discover new parts in the atom and new functions. Just the same, they maintain that it's all an accident. They've gotten a new idol which they call evolution. They ascribe more miracles to that evolution than you can find in all the books about saints in all the religions. It's good for their rapacious business. Since there is no God, no plan, no purpose, you can hit and cheat and kill with a clean conscience."

"What is your God?" I asked. "A heavenly wolf?"

"Yes, a cosmic wolf, the dictator of all dictators. It is all His work: the hungry wolf, the frightened sheep, the struggle for existence, the cancers, the heart attacks, insanity. He created them all, Hitler, Stalin, Khmelnitski, and Petlyura. It is said that He creates new angels every day. They flatter Him, sing odes to Him, and then they are liquidated, just like the old Bolsheviks."

He became quiet, and I inscribed all the adult books, all the children's books, and all his magazines. "Where did you get all this?" I asked.

"I bought it, I didn't steal it," he said. "When I can save up a few dollars I buy books, not only yours; mostly scientific ones."

"But you don't believe in the scientists," I said.

"Not in their cosmology and sociology."

"If you'd like, you can leave me some of your manuscripts," I said. "I'd be glad to read some of your poems."

My guest hesitated for a while. "What for? It's not necessary."

"I feel that you have talent," I said. "Who knows? You may be a great poet."

"No, no, not by any measurement. A man has to be something and I dabble in poetry. Thank you for the good words anyhow. Who needs poetry in our times? Not even the poets."

"There are some who need it."

"No."

My guest stretched out one hand to me and with the other began to push his wagon. I accompanied him to the door. I proposed to him again that I would like to read his works, and he said, "I thank you very much. What can poetry do? Nothing. There were quite a number of poets among the Nazis. In the day they dragged out children from their cribs and burned them and at night they wrote poems. Believe me, these two actions don't contradict one another. Absolutely not. Good night."

Translated by the author and Lester Goran

THE SECRET

She was a tiny old woman with freshly dyed pitch-black hair, a little wrinkled face, and black eyes which gleamed with a youthful zeal. She leaned on a cane, gave me a coquettish smile, and revealed a mouthful of small false teeth. Her Yiddish was rich with all the mannerisms and intonations of the Lublin region. She was saying, "I read every word you write. I never miss your advice on the radio. It's been weeks that I've tried to contact you, but you're impossible to reach on the telephone. Where do you run around the whole day? Excuse me for being so familiar with you. You don't know me, but I know you like a brother."

I thanked her and offered her a seat. She handed me her cane and I stood it in a corner. The seat was too high for her, so I put a telephone book down in place of a footstool. She said, "You are looking at an old woman, but how long has it been since I've been young? In one of your articles you mentioned a poet—I have forgotten his name—who said, 'Old people die young.' Golden words. This old person who sits before you will die a young girl. The soul does not age. In a way my memory becomes younger from day to day. What happened yesterday I forget, but things which occurred sixty years ago linger before my eyes. I have an unbelievable story for you. A story like this happens once in a thousand years."

"Do you want to tell me a story or seek advice?" I asked.

"Both. But you must be patient."

"Do me a favor and make it short." I said.

"Short, huh? How can someone make fifty or sixty years short? But I will try. I am not just a nobody. My father was a scribe. He transcribed Torah scrolls, phylacteries, *mezuzahs*, and we girls—we were four daughters and one son—tried to copy his script, not on parchment but on paper. I whittled the goose-feather quills for him and lined the parchment sheets. Our mother was a learned woman, and she taught us the Bible. I could sit with you seven days and seven nights and still not tell a fraction of what I lived through, but today people have no patience. I was also quick when I was young. What's the rush? I won't be late for the grave.

"Our father, Reb Moshe the scribe, as he was called, was a saintly Jew. His father, Reb Yerucham—also a scribe—was of such piety that before he would transcribe a holy name he went to the ritual bath. In certain sections of the Pentateuch God's name is mentioned at every line and he went from the parchment scroll to the ritual bath and back to his parchment scroll. It took him twenty years to transcribe a complete Torah scroll and weeks to write sections of the phylacteries. He and his family would have died from hunger, but our grandmother, Tirtza Perl, had a small store. She was married at fourteen and had seventeen children in her lifetime. I remember her being pregnant even when she was a grandmother. She and my mother always went around with bellies. From the seventeen children my grandmother bore, eleven died. This grandmother was the type of housewife one doesn't find in our time. She worked in the store, cooked, baked, did the wash, and even chopped wood if necessary. She prepared for the Passover while carrying a child in her arms. I will never understand where they found the strength. That was my maternal grandmother; the other grandmother died young.

"Being the oldest, I had to help my mother carry the burden of raising the younger children. There was no time to develop friendships. I was an ardent reader of literature. My brother Shmuel Chaim had secretly read Isaac Meir Dick and Mendele Mokher Seforim and along with older boys had subscribed to a Yiddish newspaper from Warsaw, and I read it too. Here in America I read your works and I know that you understand the human soul. I want to tell you something that I never told anyone before. I was secretly very passionate and I began to think about love very very early. I understood a great deal, but I didn't want to worry my parents. We sisters read Shomer's novels. There was a maid in our town, the daughter of a water-carrier, who was impregnated by a Cossack. There were many Cossacks in the village and they often went to a nearby brothel behind the Russian cemetery. Boys went there in the dark when the moon wasn't shining. There were nights when I would lie awake and break out in a cold sweat musing about these things.

"In America people have forgotten what went on in the old country. The young generation doesn't know how good they have it here. Every year after the Feast of Tabernacles an epidemic spread through the town. We had a grave-digger who was nicknamed Gehenna's Beadle. When the little children began to die he went and collected the little corpses, wrapped each one in a piece of linen from a torn bed sheet or a shirt, and he buried them himself. I'm sorry to say it, but he was a drunkard like all the members of the Burial Society. On the way to the cemetery he used to stop off at the tavern. Once, he left a sack of tiny bodies on a bench. There was such a hue and cry in the town that he was dismissed.

"Both my parents died before their time and within the same year. After they passed away, the younger children—our brother Shmuel Chaim and my three sisters—scattered in all directions. One went to serve as a maid in Lublin, another married a Litvak who took her to Russia. Eventually, Shmuel Chaim ended up in America. They are no longer among the living. Look at what I've become—a broken shard. I was once a pretty girl. In those times a girl had to have a dowry. My aunt, Chaye Gutshe, had taken responsibility for me. When people proposed a match for me, she came to examine the man. My dear writer, she married me off to a tailor, a widower, who was over forty years my senior, a father and grandfather. He already had a gray beard when we stood under the wedding canopy. I thought to myself, 'He's a man, it's better than having nobody.' I'd rather not mention his name or the town we came from. When you hear the whole story you will understand why.

"We married. He was a pious Jew, a decent man, but nothing else. I had hoped to have a child, even a few children, but a number of years passed and I did not become pregnant. With us Jews, what is a woman worth without children? The thought that I was a barren woman, or wombless as they say, was a blow. My husband may have become sterile in his old age."

"A man doesn't become sterile in his old age," I said. "He may only become impotent."

"Huh? This he was not. But he was nothing to rave about, either. He waited for me to go to the ritual bath every month and only then did he come to me. He was a men's tailor and mostly made long gaberdines. He was unusually observant. Six o'clock in the morning he went to pray. They made him a trustee in the small tailor's shul. He also led the congregation in prayer. His only worry was that my matron's wig would slip somewhat and men would see my hair and fall into sinful thoughts. His one worker was also an elderly man. I cooked for both men and carried water from the well. My life was as good as over, but I made peace with it. My husband constantly spoke of saving money. In order to live honestly one must always have something saved for hard times. We saved what we could. I was only spend-thrifty when it came to books. When a book-peddler came to town I bought whatever was available in Yiddish: storybooks, a novel from Isaac Meir Dick, Shlomo Ettinger, Mendele Mokher Seforim, Sholem Aleichem, Peretz, Sholom Asch. A small Yiddish library was established in our village and I could secretly get books there. My husband spat on worldly books, calling them heretical. But reading was the only pleasure left to me. My brother Shmuel Chaim sometimes sent me books from

America: Zeyfert, Shomer, Kubrin, Libin. I cannot describe the satisfaction I got from reading these books. They literally saved my life.

"Now the real story begins. Once my husband brought home an apprentice called Motke. He was a boy of thirteen from a nearby shtetl. I say thirteen because I remember when he put on phylacteries for the Bar Mitzvah. The other tailors kept their apprentices like slaves. They ran errands, brought water from the pump, poured out the slop pail, and rocked the babies in their cradles. These boys were only given food and a night's lodging on top of the stove. The contract was signed by the boy's father or by a relative if he was an orphan. Many tailors cheated the boys. Months went by before they taught them to cut out a hole or sew on a button.

"Motke was an orphan and I don't remember whether my husband wrote out a contract for him or simply made a verbal agreement. My husband was honest and immediately began teaching Motke the trade. This Motke was clever and had golden hands. He grasped everything quickly and my husband praised him to Heaven. What was he like? He was dark with black eyes, clever with a sense of humor like none other in the world. Little jokes poured out of him which always made me laugh. He could read and soon indulged in my books.

"My husband always protected him, warned me not to overwork the boy, take advantage of him, God forbid. Who wanted to take advantage? I cooked the meals he liked and treated him like an only son. He said that I was like a mother and that my husband was like a father to him. The other tailors complained that we pampered him and that if other apprentices were to hear of the comfort he enjoyed with us, they would rebel and demand higher wages.

"Times were changing. Strikes had begun in Russia. Workers were beginning to revolt, carrying revolvers and throwing bombs. The Czar had been shot only a few years earlier. We were a little town in the hinterland, but there were already those youths who sought equality for all. They met after the Sabbath meal in the woods and organized what they called a circle. A few apprentices secretly joined the group but Motke said he would never join. How could he have complained when we provided him with the best of everything? He made fun of their petitions to the government and revolutionary proclamations. He boasted that when he learned the trade he would himself become an employer. He wanted to become a ladies' tailor, sew jackets and dresses for pretty girls, not gaberdines for Chassidim. He was a big talker."

"You fell in love with him, huh?" I asked.

The old woman was quiet for a long while. "One should not eat kugel with you," she said.

"Why not?"

"Because you grab things too quickly. Yes, you are right. I saw that he looked at me constantly. Once in a while he stole a kiss. I pleaded with him not to, but he listened to me like Haman listens to the Purim-grogger. He was ready to sow his wild oats. He often behaved like a fully ripe man. I considered telling my husband, who would have surely chased him out in disgrace. But I had grown attached to him. My dear man, since you are guessing things, what's the use of trying to deny them? Yes, he became my lover."

"When did it happen? How?"

"One summer, on a Sabbath. It could never have happened in the middle of the week, since my husband worked at home. But on Sabbath afternoon he used to go to the tailors' study group, to study *The Ethics of the Fathers*. Later, the congregation recited the evening prayer and ate the third meal, which consisted of stale challah and herring. Afterwards, they recited the Havdalah and sang valedictory songs. By the time he came home it was already late in the evening. I used to read in bed after the Sabbath meal. That day I had fallen into a deep sleep. I opened my eyes and Motke was lying beside me in bed. I wanted to scream in alarm, but he closed my mouth with his hand like an experienced rascal. This was a devil, not an apprentice."

"Is this the whole story?" I asked.

"Just the beginning."

We sat in silence for a long while. It seemed to me the old woman's face had become younger and less wrinkled. Something of a smile appeared in her eyes. Only her head, with its black hair—dulled from the dye—trembled like an old woman's. Then she said:

"It happened, and it's too late for regret now. I acted like a mother, but he treated me like a wife. At times our conduct seemed utterly sinful and ugly to me—a humiliation beyond words to us and to my parents in Paradise. He also had parents in the other world, and I felt terribly degraded before them too. I tried with all my power to drive him away, but he wouldn't hear of it. Although nobody visited us during the day on the Sabbath, still, what would I have done had the door opened and someone would have come in? I would have died on the spot. How I wish this would have really happened, because what followed was worse than death."

"You became pregnant, huh?"

The woman's face became harsh and hostile. "God in Heaven, I'm afraid of you! What are you? A mind reader?"

"I simply understand."

"Yes, it happened. But not immediately. He remained with us over two years. I had gotten so accustomed to him that I could no longer live without him. The entire week I looked forward to the Sabbath. A holy day, and I defiled it with such abominations. In the meantime he became taller, broader, a real man. I cannot describe how good he was at tailoring; how adept at sewing on the machine—which we later acquired. He helped my husband cut out material and took measurements. He held a piece of chalk in hand and did everything with speed and precision like a master tailor. Our worker saw that he was no longer needed and left. The tailors became my husband's blood enemies. It was against the rules to train an apprentice so quickly. Their notions dated back to King Sobieski's time—to keep an apprentice for three years without pay and afterwards begin by paying him half a ruble a month. I will make it short. One day Motke said that he was planning to go to Warsaw. The moment he mentioned Warsaw I knew I had lost him. For me this was a black day.

"Where was I, heh? Yes, said and done. My husband tried to talk him into staying with us, but with him a word was a deed. I yearned for him. The week days were still bearable, but when the Sabbath came I felt the pain. He promised to send a card, but it never came. This is what men are, egotists, young and old. Excuse me for speaking this way about your gender. It is not their fault, it's their nature. Weeks passed, months. Suddenly, it dawned on me that I hadn't gotten my period, or the 'holiday,' as we called it, for some time. When this occurred to me I knew I was going to become a mother and who the father was."

"How could you have known?" I asked. "You lived with two men."

"I knew. I would have normally rejoiced at becoming a mother. My aunt always said, 'A wife without children is like a tree without fruit.' But to have a child out of wedlock, and with a young boy at that, was a sin which God would not forgive and a woman, unless she is a whore, cannot bear. I seriously considered suicide, but I could not bring myself to do it. I had compassion for my husband, who became helpless after Motke left. His old age had descended upon him suddenly. He seemed sick to me. He had become half deaf, and I had to repeat every word I said to him. He had difficulties in threading a needle. His customers began to complain, 'The gaberdine is too long, too short, too narrow.' You should excuse my frankness, but he made a pair of pants and the crotch came out too high or too low. In the middle of all this I had to bring him the tidings that I was pregnant. He was a devout Jew and he took the news as a gift from God, but I could see very well that he didn't feel this way. Who wants to become a father in their old age? Nobody, God forbid, suspected anything. In that time such a disgrace never happened even among the lowest. What a crime to deliver a bastard to a husband!

God in Heaven, my days were hell and at night I shook in bed as if in a fever. I begged God to let me miscarry. I had heard that if you drink vinegar or jump off a table it can help and I tried this at every opportunity, but to no avail. It was already too late. Well, I had a girl, not a boy. Usually, people want a boy, but in this situation it's better to have a girl. If she gets married she no longer carries and defiles her father's name.

"My husband only lived four years after her birth and he loved her more than his other children. I know what you want to ask, 'How could I be sure who the father was?' In the beginning I knew because my heart told me so. When she was born I didn't need to rely on my heart. She looked exactly like Motke: his eyes, his ears, the shape of his mouth. I shuddered with fear that people would notice the resemblance and there would be a terrible scandal. But thank God, no one suspected anything. Only I, the debased mother, could see the bitter truth."

"How old is your daughter?" I asked.

The woman was taken aback. "What? She is forty-five years old, but you wouldn't take her for more than thirty. A beauty and educated as well. She is a teacher of mathematics in a high school and they wanted to make her a professor in a college."

"When did you come to America?" I asked.

"Thirty-seven years ago, a few years before Hitler's slaughter. My brother, Shmuel Chaim, or Sam as they called him here, saved me. He had become rich in America and sent me an affidavit. When I came here he was better to me than a father."

"Is your daughter married?"

"Was. Twice. She is divorced."

"And did you marry again?"

"Yes, also twice, already here in America. Both my husbands died. With one I only lived two years. With the other one I lived thirteen years, and he died close to ninety. He left me a lot of money, but what good is money to me at this age? It is all for my daughter."

"Is that everything?"

"Wait, my dear man, this is still not the main thing I wanted to tell you. As I said, what happened to me can only happen once in a thousand years, or possibly in a million years."

"What happened to you?"

The old woman did not answer. Her lips quivered. She tried to speak, but she choked on the words. Finally, she cried out, "My daughter lives with her father! He is her lover. They are planning to marry!"

Some time passed before the woman found her tongue. She looked at me with wrath as if I were to blame for this occurrence. She called out, "I, alone, am the cause of this abomination! Only I and nobody else!"

"Your daughter . . ."

The old woman interrupted me, "She knew nothing and knows nothing. I had mentioned to her that we once had an apprentice, Motke, and that's all she knows. She came to America with me when she was still a young girl. She didn't know a word of English. I sent her to school. My brother, may he rest in peace, helped me and she immediately took to her studies. She was the best student in her class, and it continued in this way every year. She finished high school at seventeen. She remembered my husband, her supposed father, she remembered him. She had a fantastic memory. What she couldn't recall she asked me. She wanted to know every detail about him. Such love from a child to a father who died somewhere in the old country before she was even five years old always struck me as strange. Here in America children have little feeling for immigrant parents, especially if they are brought up without a father. But Sylvia—this is the American name my brother gave her, her real name is Sarah Leah—often probed and questioned me. We only had one photograph from his Polish passport and she persuaded me to make a large portrait from it and frame it, hang it over her bed. I didn't want to talk about him too much, and I didn't actually have that much to tell. But she simply exhausted me with her inquiries year in, year out. When I remarried she was angry with me, and when I married again, she became my enemy. What could I do? In the old country I was dead. Here, I came back to life. I went to night school and learned English. I went to the Yiddish theater and later to the English theater as well. I loved my child more than my own life, but she had waged war with me and I knew this was a punishment from God. We had relatives here, all living in Brooklyn. I once had a job with Abraham and Straus and I became their first sales-lady. When I married for the second time and I gave up the job, they made a banquet for me.

"Now about my daughter. She is clever, pretty, edu-cated. She resembles her father—her real father—like two drops of water. But she had no luck with men. She was married twice and it was wrong both times. Neither of these men wanted children. She was dying to have a child, but there was no one around. It was just her bad luck that men were always coarse with her, even brutal. My dear man, there is a lot to tell. At times I thought that in body she was from her real father and her soul was from my first husband. You frequently write about dybbuks, mysterious things. Can it be that my first husband's soul entered her after his death?"

"Everything is possible."

"Ah, the world is full of secrets. I have to tell you something which has to do with your writing. When I came to America I began to read the *Forward*, and this opened up the world to me. I was hospitalized twice in my life and my daughter had to bring the *Forward* to me every day. She also learned to read Yiddish and wrote an essay on its literature in college. My daughter listens to you on the radio and . . ."

"When and how did you meet Motke?" I asked.

"It happened suddenly, like all misfortunes. We were shopping for bargains on Orchard Street at the pushcarts. We didn't find what we were looking for, but we got hungry and went for supper on Second Avenue at Rappaport's restaurant. After we were sitting and eating a while a man approached our table. He was tall, well dressed. He came over and said, 'Ladies, excuse me but I must ask you something!' "

" 'What do you want to ask?' I said. And he asked, 'Aren't you from . . .' and he mentioned the name of our town.

"In New York we have a landsman society, a cemetery and all the rest of it. But for some reason I never joined. God should not punish me, but I hid from our landsmen. Many of my acquaintances had died, and the younger generation perished with the Nazis. My two husbands here were Litvaks, and they were members of their own societies. When the man mentioned the name of our town, I wanted to say no, but I am not a liar by nature and answered yes. My daughter became all ears. She often confronted me about avoiding my landsmen. For her it was a sign that I was trying to forget her father. The man told us he came to America many years ago and became a rich garment manufacturer here. His wife died of cancer. I will tell you something and you won't believe me. I took one look at him and at my daughter and I knew that I had fallen into a trap from which one cannot emerge alive."

"Why didn't you tell Sylvia that he was her father?" I asked.

"Because I knew and I know to this day that if she would have to go through another disappointment, it would be her death," the old woman answered. "I fear God, but I don't want to lose my daughter."

"Why didn't it occur to him, since she resembles him so much?" I asked.

The old woman did not answer. She lowered her head and was silent. Then she said, "Who knows if it did occur to him or not? He made it clear to me that very night that he was an atheist. When my daughter was washing her hands in the ladies' room I made him swear to me that he would never say a word to her about what had passed between us and he promised me. He took the whole thing lightly. He sat with us three hours and only talked about his successes in business and with women. He had a son from a previous wife. He had a house on Long Island and an apartment on West End Avenue. People knew him well in Rappaport's; they even called him to the telephone. He wouldn't let us pay for supper and left a three-dollar tip. He made a date with my daughter on the spot. When he had entered the restaurant my daughter seemed tired, pale, old for her age. But when he drove us home in his Cadillac to Brooklyn, my daughter looked and spoke like a young girl. A mother understands such things. It was, as they say, love at first sight. She sat next to him in the front. I sat in the back and saw how he drove the car with his left hand. His right hand he already kept on her lap. She turned her head to me and said out loud, 'Mama, I found my father.' Those were her words. She didn't know herself that she spoke the truth. My heart tightened as if a fist would clamp down on it with all its strength. I thought my end had come, but those who want to live, die. And those who want to die often live to be a hundred years."

"My dear lady, with such problems one goes to a rabbi or to a psychiatrist, not to a writer," I said. "You know yourself that I cannot help you."

"Yes, I know. But who can help me? I had one comfort: that she was already too old to have children. At least she would not give birth to a bastard. But lately she began to say that she is prepared to risk everything in order to become pregnant. I have only one hope, that I will not live through the shame and the degradation."

"The world is full of illegitimate children," I said.

"Not from a father with his own daughter. People didn't commit such inquities even in the time of the Flood," the old woman said.

She made a gesture to leave and I brought her the cane.

She leaned on it heavily, wobbled, and balanced herself in order not to fall.

"Come, I will lead you," I said as I held her by the shoulders.

"Please wait a minute. When I sit too long in one place my legs get stiff," she said. "The blood no longer flows easily through my veins. My limbs are all sick, but my mind is clear. I thought that since she reads everything you write and worships you, maybe you could discourage her from this man."

"I would not be able to, nor would I want to. If God wants a kosher world, He will have to create one Himself."

"I am afraid He, too, would not know what to do in this case," the old woman said.

She smiled, and for a split second her face became young again.

Translated by Deborah Menashe

A NEST EGG
FOR PARADISE

I t all happened in the city of Lublin. Two brothers lived there who jointly owned a fabric shop, considered to be the finest in the province. The wealthiest landowners, and even the governor and his wife, used to shop there for their fabrics.

The elder brother, Reb Mendel, had the reputation of a scholar. He was also a follower of the Chassidic master Reb Bunem of Przysucha. Because Reb Mendel was always absorbed in study and in Chassidic lore, he had little time left to devote to business. Both in his appearance and his character Reb Mendel resembled his father, Reb Gershon of blessed memory: tall and broad, his beard and sidelocks black, his manner always gentle. The younger brother, Joel, was small, not given to learning, and a clown by nature. Joel had flaming red hair, a red little beard, and no hint of sidelocks. Whatever Joel did, he did in a hurry. He didn't walk, he ran. He spoke in a hurry, ate in a hurry, he rushed through his prayers. One minute he rose to recite the Eighteen Benedictions, the next he was done. He put on his prayer shawl and phylacteries, then promptly took them off. Because Joel had a flair for business, and because he liked to travel to all the great fairs where he met buyers and traders from every corner of Poland and sometimes from other countries as well, Reb Mendel had drawn up a written agreement allotting sixty percent of the profits to Joel and taking the remaining forty percent himself. Basha-Meitl, Mendel's wife, fretted a good deal over her husband's agreement. Basha-Meitl had borne her husband three girls and a boy, while Lisa-Hadas, her sister-in-law, had borne Joel no children. Since the couple was childless after ten years of married life, Jewish law required Joel to divorce his wife. But Joel refused. When people asked him why he did not heed the law, Joel would answer with a joke, "I already expect a good lashing in hell. Let there be a few lashes more."

Another time he said, "If I divorced Lisa-Hadas every widow, spinster, and divorcee would be after me to marry her. I'd never know which one to choose. Staying married is the best protection for a fellow like me."

By the time he was forty-five Reb Mendel had married off all his children. He could not provide large dowries for his daughters, but because they were pretty and well brought-up, they found themselves good husbands. Basha-Meitl often complained to Reb Mendel that had he not been so immersed in Chassidic lore and practice—often spending more time in Przysucha than at home—he could have found himself more prosperous sons-in-law. But Reb Mendel would answer, "When a man reaches the world to come and is required to render accounts, the angel does not ask him how rich or poor are his sons-in-law. He asks instead, 'Did you study Torah? Was your business honorable?' "

It was the custom for Joel to send Reb Mendel his portion of the week's profits on Friday. Joel never offered to show Reb Mendel his account books, and Reb Mendel never asked to see them. Although the shop had grown steadily larger and Joel had taken on additional help, and although the shelves had been stacked from floor to ceiling with the finest merchandise, the earnings, it seemed, remained more or less the same. Basha-Meitl often nagged her husband to demand a precise accounting of expenses and profits. But Reb Mendel refused, saying, "If I can't trust my own brother, whom then can I trust? And if, God forbid, he is a swindler—what's to prevent him from falsifying the books?" And he made Basha-Meitl solemnly promise never to bring up these ugly suspicions again.

"What do they want with so much money?" Basha-Meitl would ask. "To whom will they leave their fortune?"

And Reb Mendel would answer, "With the Almighty's help they'll live to a hundred and twenty."

As different as were the two brothers so also were their wives. Reb Mendel's wife, Basha-Meitl, was the same age as he. A pious woman, she wore a double bonnet on her shaved head, so that when the hair on her head began to grow out again it would not be seen, God forbid, by a stranger's eye because it is written, "A woman's hair is akin to her nakedness." Basha-Meitl fasted not only on Yom Kippur and the Ninth of Av, as the other women did, but also on the Seventeenth of Tammuz, the Fast of Esther, and the Tenth of Tevet, as well as the eight Fridays of the Shovavim Tat in the winter—which was only a custom and not a commanded law. Every Sabbath she read the weekly portion in the Yiddish Pentateuch, and she often read (in Yiddish translation) the *Good Heart*, the *Rod of Punish-*

ment, the *Lamp of Light*, and the *Right Measure*. Frugal by nature, she had managed to put aside a small nest egg, so that come what may neither she nor her husband should have to come begging, God forbid, to their children, let alone to strangers. Both she and Reb Mendel had written a will leaving one half of their savings to the children and the other to various charities—to the poorhouse, for marrying off poor or orphaned brides, to the old-age home and the orphanage.

Joel's wife was ten years younger than her husband. Spared the pains of childbirth and child rearing she looked younger still. Lisa-Hadas indulged herself in every luxury. She did no housework at all, employing instead two maids. She had a sweet tooth and was forever nibbling cookies, cakes, strudels, sipping sweet liqueurs or cherry brandy. Instead of a bonnet she wore a wig, whose hair she combed so that it blended with her own. Lisa-Hadas was the same height as Joel, and as quick and nimble as he. She flew about on her high-heeled shoes, darting here and there like a bird. Although many dresses, blouses, robes, and coats filled her closets, she always complained of having nothing to wear and spent long hours with her tailors and seamstresses. She had a chest filled with shoes of every color and another with hats topped with silk flowers, with ostrich plumes, with wooden peaches, pomegranates, bunches of grapes. Whenever Joel traveled, he returned with a piece of jewelry for her: a necklace, a brooch, a ring, earrings. Lisa-Hadas attended the synagogue only on the High Holidays, or on those occasions when she happened to escort a bride to her wedding. Like her husband Lisa-Hadas was forever ready with a joke. Her high-pitched laughter often ended with a squeal. When she went to the ritual bath at the end of her menstrual periods, the other wives had much to envy her for. She'd come all decked out in silk lingerie edged in exquisite lace, long stockings which reached up to her thighs. Her breasts were firm and pointed like a girl's. The younger women showered her with compliments, but the older ones acidly asked her, "What is it with you, Lisa-Hadas, not getting any older?" And Lisa-Hadas would answer with a wink, "I have a potion which keeps whomever drinks it young till ninety."

There had been a time when Reb Mendel used to spend several hours in the shop every week, so that he might not become completely estranged either from the business or from Joel. But that time had long since gone. Joel had taken on clerks to help him wait on customers and to run the shop for him when he traveled. Women's fashions and styles were constantly changing. One year dresses hung loose, the next they clung to the body. One year lapels were narrow, the next they were wide. There was no sense in paying attention to such vanity. Besides, Reb Mendel was glad to avoid running into his sister-in-law. Lisa-Hadas had become a fashion expert. She subscribed to magazines which came to her from far-off Paris—that bit of Sodom whose women were forever occupied with finding new ways to titillate men. Napoleon, who was said to have been the vicious Gog, or perhaps the Magog mentioned in the Bible, had been defeated in one of his battles and had died on some bleak and forsaken island. But still the world craved nothing better than to ape the French, to speak their language, to imitate their whims and caprices. In the larger cities pious Jews had their daughters taught to prattle in French and to play on the piano. The Enlightenment, which had begun in Germany with that heretic Moses Mendelssohn Dessauer, soon drifted over to Russia and even to Poland. In Vienna and in Berlin and Budapest cropped up Reform synagogues, where *rabbiners* delivered their sermons in German, and where an organ was played on the Sabbath and holidays. Secular writers repeated in their Hebrew magazines every blasphemous theory put forth by the philosophers. They denied the miraculous nature of the Exodus from Egypt, as well as the divinity of the Torah. Reb Mendel suspected that secretly Lisa-Hadas belonged in their camp. He did not even trust the *kashruth* of her household, because she let it be run by Gentile servants.

After he stopped going to the shop, Reb Mendel studied the Talmud and Chassidic books at the prayer house in Lublin every afternoon after his nap. Lublin was a city of Chassidim. When The Seer, Rabbi Yaakov Yitzhak, had been alive, Chassidim from every corner of Poland flocked to Lublin. After The Seer's death, his disciple Bunem of Przysucha had taken his place. Reb Bunem did not perform miracles, as had The Seer. Reb Bunem's way in Chassidism was the way of wisdom. He assembled around him a select circle of scholars, keen minds, young men in search of a new way in Chassidism. Reb Bunem was fluent in Polish, even in Russian. He had been a pharmacist at one time. His adversaries, the *Mitnagdim*, denounced him. Even among the Chassidim there were those who thought him too clever, too blunt, and thought that some of his utterances smacked of heresy. But those who understood a thing or two could glean layers upon layers of mysteries from his words.

One summer afternoon, as Reb Mendel sat alone in the study house poring over some sacred volume, the door was pushed open a crack. Reb Mendel looked up, and standing in the doorway he saw his sister-in-law, Lisa-Hadas. She was dressed in a cream-colored suit topped with a straw hat and a ribbon. In one hand she carried a handbag and in the other a white parasol such as were carried by the wives of the rich landowners to shield themselves from the sun. So startled was Reb Mendel by her presence that he dropped the book to the floor. Something's happened to my brother, was the thought that raced through his head. He stood up and said, "Do my eyes deceive me?"

"No, Mendel. It's me, your sister-in-law, Lisa-Hadas."

"What brings you here?" he asked, with a tremor in his voice.

"I looked for you at your house, but the maid told me you were here."

"What happened? Is something, God forbid, wrong with Joel?"

"Yes. Something is wrong with Joel. But don't be alarmed. He's alive."

"Taken ill, God forbid?"

"I can't talk here."

"Where, then?"

"Come home with me."

"Home, with you?"

"Yes, why not? It isn't far. I'm not a stranger to you, Mendel. I am still your brother's wife."

"Is Joel back in Lublin?"

"Joel is still in Cracow."

Lisa-Hadas spoke to Reb Mendel with a mixture of impudence and mockery, born of familiarity. Reb Mendel had never walked with a woman in public before, not even with Basha-Meitl. When once it had happened that they had gone somewhere together, he had walked out in front and she had followed behind him. He had always been mindful of the words in the Gemara: "Better follow a lion than a woman." He had also remembered the words "Manoach was a simpleton, as it is written: 'And Manoach walked behind his wife.'"

"Can't you tell me here what has happened to my brother?" Reb Mendel asked.

"No."

Reb Mendel hesitated before he followed Lisa-Hadas out of the prayer house, and then he walked half beside her and half in front. He cast furtive glances at passers-by to see whether they noticed him or pointed their fingers at him.

He muttered, "What's keeping Joel in Cracow?"

"You'll know soon," Lisa-Hadas answered.

Before long they arrived at his brother's house. Reb Mendel had not been to the house in years. Lisa-Hadas had had a garden planted in front, and as he approached Reb Mendel saw large sunflowers in bloom. She had also had a balcony added to the second story. Lisa-Hadas grabbed the large brass ring which hung on the door and knocked several times. A Gentile maid in a white apron and a starched bonnet appeared to let them in. "Real squires," Reb Mendel thought to himself. An oriental carpet covered the floor of the front foyer. Two bronze figures holding lanterns stood facing one another. Lisa-Hadas led him into a living room crowded with sofas, stuffed chairs, paintings, chandeliers, pots filled with plants such as Mendel had never seen and for which the Yiddish he spoke had no names. She showed him to a sofa upholstered in black velvet, then sat herself on a chair opposite him and propped her feet on an embroidered stool. She said, "Mendel, I hate to be the bearer of bad news, but your brother has become a *goy*."

Reb Mendel turned pale. "Not converted, God forbid?"

"I don't know. Perhaps not yet. But he's got himself a Gentile mistress."

Reb Mendel felt his mouth turn dry and his stomach tighten. For a moment he was out of breath. "How can this be? I can't believe it," he stammered.

"I found a whole stack of her letters to him. He supports her. He showers her with gifts and money. It's been going on for over five years."

"Somehow I can't bring myself to believe all this."

"I'll show you her letters. You understand Polish, don't you?"

"A little."

"When your brother and I were first married you used to come to the shop every day and, as I remember, you spoke with the landowners and their wives in a rather fluent Polish."

"*Nu.*"

For a while both sat silent. Reb Mendel glanced at his sister-in-law and wondered why he had taken in her news without a greater show of grief. He was not a whiner by nature. He had not cried even at his parents' funerals. He had often seen Jews sobbing on Yom Kippur during the

Kol Nidre or on the Ninth of Av during the Lamentations, but it was not in his nature to shed tears. He always kept in mind the verse: "I stand ever ready for adversity, and my woes are always on my mind." He prepared himself for whatever might befall him. The children, God forbid, might die; he, Mendel, might suddenly take ill or Basha-Meitl might be taken from him, leaving him a widower. How did the saying go? "There is not a moment without its woe." And yet, that his brother Joel, their parents' youngest born, should sink to such depths—for that he was unprepared. He heard Lisa-Hadas speaking to him, "Mendel, since we are in the midst of speaking the truth, let me confess the whole truth."

"And what is that?"

"The truth is that Joel was not honest with you. You were supposed to receive forty percent of the profits, but in all those years you received not forty, nor thirty, nor even twenty percent. He is your brother while I am only an outsider—what, after all, is a sister-in-law?—but I confronted him with this I don't know how many times, and his answer was always the same: you are an idler, impractical, old-fashioned and stubborn, you don't lift a finger to help, and so on and so forth. I told him: 'Mendel could do plenty, but you drove him out of the shop, you kept things from him, you excluded him from everything.' A wife should not denounce her husband, but if he's taking up with a *shikse* and makes a fool of me—I owe him nothing. Am I right or am I wrong?"

"*Nu.*"

"All these years I have been faithful to him. I could have had more lovers than I have hairs on my head. Men lose their heads over me, but I've always believed in one God and one husband. Now it's all over. He is no longer my husband and I am not his wife. Let me tell you something, Mendel. You may not believe this, but you are closer to me now than he ever was. You are honest while he is a thief. When he and I were first married, you were the accomplished merchant while he was nothing but mama's pampered little boy. I was barely fourteen then, but I remember: From the very beginning he tried to take everything over and to push you out. I know, Mendel, that you disapprove of me because I'm not one of those overly pious matrons and I like to comb my wigs in the modern way. But I've always had the greatest respect for you. Don't laugh, but even as a man I preferred you to him. When my father, may he rest in peace, used to recite the Havdalah at the close of the Sabbath my mother would hand me the Havdalah-candle and say: 'Hold it high, and you'll have a tall husband.' When I became engaged and the people gathered to draw up the marriage contract I thought it was you I was marrying. I was a child then, not more than fourteen. But when I saw that my bridegroom was short, shorter than me, a mere boy and not a young man—my heart sank. Why am I telling you all this? Because my heart is heavy now, and because I have no children, no heirs. I want you to know, Mendel, that it is Joel's fault that we are childless, not mine. I could have had a dozen children if I had married a man instead of a barren tree."

"How can you be so sure?" Mendel asked.

"A doctor told me. An obstetrician, that's what they call themselves. He examined me head to toe. 'You, Lisa-Hadas, are a healthy female,' he said to me. Those were his very words. 'It's your husband's fault, not yours.' What shall I do, brother-in-law? What shall I do now?" Lisa-Hadas cried out in a singsong voice.

Reb Mendel wanted to answer, but his tongue refused to obey him. A lump rose up to his throat. He made an attempt to swallow the lump, then he heard his own voice saying, "For the time being do nothing. Wait until Joel returns."

"His return frightens me. I won't be able to look him straight in the eye. He'll be coming to me from the arms of that whore, from her unclean body. Mendel, what is the matter? You're as pale as a ghost. Wait, I'll get something for you."

She sprang out of her chair, ran up to a cabinet and flung open its glass doors. She pulled out a bottle half filled with a reddish fluid and poured from it into a polished glass. In a moment she was back at his side. "Here, drink this," she said. "It's sweet liqueur, for women. Let me get you something to nibble on."

Reb Mendel held the glass tightly in his hand, but his hand shook so violently that it was several minutes before he could touch it to his lips. He poured the liquid into his mouth and felt a sharp burning in his tongue, his palate, his throat. Lisa-Hadas returned carrying another glass and a plate heaped with cookies. "Drink, Mendel," she said. "I know what a shock this must be for you. I had misplaced a ring of mine, and I thought I might have hidden it in one of his drawers. I opened the drawer and saw her pack of letters bulging out from under his papers. That night I didn't sleep a wink. I lay in my bed and shivered as if in a fever. I thought of hanging myself, of taking poison."

"God forbid. You'd be committing a grave sin." Reb Mendel could hardly pronounce the words.

"How grave can it be? I considered it all very carefully. There is no God."

"What are you saying? This is blasphemy!"

"Let it be blasphemy. Don't worry, Mendel. It's I who will roast in the fires of Hell, not you. Come, let me show you those brazen letters of hers."

Reb Mendel wanted to rise, but it was as if he were paralyzed. Lisa-Hadas took his hands in hers and helped him to his feet. His knees struck against hers. A shudder ran through his spine, and for a moment he was overcome by lust such as he had not known since the days of his youth. Lisa-Hadas pulled him along by both his hands, she stepping gingerly backward and he stumbling forward half-blind, shaky and trembling in a sort of drunken minuet. "Master of the Universe, help me!" a voice within him cried. Suddenly Lisa-Hadas lurched backward and fell, pulling him down to the floor. Reb Mendel had no time to grasp what happened. He tried to tear himself away from her; he had fallen into something like a swoon—an instant of sheer drunkenness and utter helplessness. She did something to him and he could not resist. He shuddered and it was as if he had awakened from a deep sleep, from a dream, from an evil force that robbed his freedom to choose. He felt as though his body had separated itself from his soul and had committed an abomination of its own accord. So dumbfounded was Reb Mendel by what had happened to him that he could not manage to shout out his grief. He lay there on the floor consumed with one wish—never to rise again. She helped him stand up and he heard her say, "He rightly deserved it." It was the voice of a Lilith: one of those female demons sent by Asmodeus to defile yeshiva students. Verses from the Book of Proverbs crowded his head: "She eats, then wipes her mouth, saying, 'I have done no wrong. . . .'" "Her feet point to the grave, her footsteps lead into the chambers of death."

Evening came, and then sudden darkness. Lisa-Hadas grasped his arm and he allowed himself to follow her like an ox to the slaughter. What was the difference anyway? Lower than the deepest abyss one couldn't sink. His knees buckled under him and his feet were unsteady. Lisa-Hadas hung on to his arm and pressed her bosom to his ribs. "Shall I have the carriage harnessed to take you home?" she asked. "First I'll have to find the groom."

"No, no."

"It's not far to your home, but it's dark outside. You could slip and fall, God forbid."

He wanted to say, "Fall still more?" but instead he said, "No, I can see."

"Basha-Meitl will wonder what's become of you." Lisa-Hadas said with a chuckle.

Reb Mendel wanted her to let him go, but for some reason she clung to him. She said, "The darkness of Egypt is out there. I'd better go with you."

"I beg you, no."

"Mendel, forgive me."

"*Nu.*"

"We both must have been out of our minds," Lisa-Hadas blurted out to him and to the night. "Be careful."

Hesitantly she let go of his arm and he set out on his way, unsteady like a drunk. "I've lost the world to come," a voice within him murmured. Everything happened in quick succession as in the Book of Job: "Even as one fellow was speaking, the second fellow arrived." Scarcely two hours ago Reb Mendel had been an honest, upstanding Jew. Now he was depraved, a Zimri Ben Salu, a betrayer of God, a lecher. If at least there would rise a Phinehas to avenge the Lord of Hosts. His, Mendel's, vision had always been adequate. He could even read the small letters in Rashi without eyeglasses. But now it was as though he had gone blind. *"Nu,* my iniquity surpasses my endurance." Words from the Gemara came rushing back to him: "May it be God's will that my death atone for my sinfulness." Someone came walking toward him, and Mendel halted. It was a young man, a Przysucha Chassid, whose name was Hershel Roizkes. Recognizing Mendel in the darkness the young man asked him, "And where might you be going at this late hour, Reb Mendel?"

Mendel didn't know what answer to give. He felt himself literally speechless.

"May I accompany you home?"

"Nu."

The young Chassid took Reb Mendel's arm, the very arm that Lisa-Hadas had earlier held, and said, "The city pays some Gentile to keep the lanterns lit, yet the streets are always dark. God forbid, a person could break a leg or even his neck. In the summertime one can tolerate it, but when winter comes with its snows and frosts and the streets become slippery, a person risks his life every time he leaves his house. You're probably planning to spend Rosh Hashanah in Przysucha, Reb Mendel, huh?"

Again Reb Mendel had no answer to give. That he,

Mendel, should present himself at the *rebbe*'s in Przysucha? It was sacrilege even to mention that saint's name in the same breath with his, adulterer that he was, an outcast to his people, disgraced and polluted. He had to answer the young Chassid's question and he murmured, "It's too early to say."

"Since you go to the *rebbe* every year, why not this time? Zeinvil the beadle predicts more disciples than ever this year," Hershel Roizkes said.

Despite his sorrow Reb Mendel couldn't help but smile to himself. Hershel was trying to engage him in Chassidic talk. How could he know that he, Mendel, was no longer Mendel but a villain seven times over, a man steeped in the Forty-Nine Gates of Uncleanliness? And how will he, Mendel, greet Basha-Meitl when finally he'll arrive at his home? How will he look her in the eye?

Hershel Roizkes was speaking of Rabbi Bunem now, repeating a saying of his, quoting a witticism, but although Reb Mendel could hear his voice, he could not make out what Hershel said. The Torah and he, Mendel, had grown estranged one from the other forever. The young man spoke up, "I see, Reb Mendel, that you are a bit impatient tonight. Are you, God forbid, ill, or what?"

"I do have a touch of heartburn."

"Huh? Right away I knew that something was wrong. You shouldn't be walking the streets at this hour. It turns quite chilly in the evening and one could easily catch a cold. Go home and get into bed. Your helpmate will give you something for it. A glass of tea with honey will cure anything. Here we are, Reb Mendel, here's your house. Good night, Reb Mendel, and may you recover soon."

"Thank you, Hershel."

When Reb Mendel opened the door to his apartment he saw Basha-Meitl standing in the middle of the room, a kerchief wrapped around her forehead. Before he had time to wish her a good evening, she began to scream, "Where have you been? Where did you run off to so late in the evening? And why are you so pale? Did something happen, God forbid? You always come home immediately after the evening prayers, and here it's already ten o'clock! The worries I've had—may they fall on our enemies' heads. The frightful disasters that came to my mind! Mendel, what is it with you? I've even developed a headache from worry."

"I lingered at the prayer house longer than I meant to."

"Mendel, I myself went to the prayer house to look for you. The beadle told me that you had not been there for the evening service."

Reb Mendel stood and stared at his wife, utterly stupefied. Heavenly Father, he had forgotten to recite the evening prayers! In all the years he'd been saying them, this had never happened to him before. "*Nu*, apparently I'm entirely in the hands of the evil host." He saw a chair and all but collapsed into it. "I'm no longer a Jew," Reb Mendel thought to himself. "It's better this way. It's better if those sacred words did not pass through my unclean lips."

"Where have you been?" Basha-Meitl shrieked at him. "You're as white as a corpse!"

Reb Mendel considered how to answer his wife. Should he make up a story? What sort of story? Fabrications and lies were not in his nature. Besides, someone might have seen him with Lisa-Hadas, walking in the direction of her house. At last he said, "I was with Lisa-Hadas."

Basha-Meitl clapped her hands together. "What? Lisa-Hadas? For such a long time? Is something wrong with your brother, God forbid?"

"Yes."

"What happened? Heaven help us! Such a young man."

"He's alive, he's alive."

"What is it then? Don't keep me in suspense!" Basha-Meitl screamed.

"Joel is having relations with a Gentile woman."

"Relations? A Gentile? I can't believe it. I can't believe it!"

"It's the truth."

"When? Where? What sort of relations?"

It occurred to Reb Mendel that he should not have spoken the word "truth." According to the Gemara, truth was the Almighty's Seal. A sinner such as he ought not to let the word cross his lips.

Man and wife talked late into the night, until finally Basha-Meitl fell asleep. Reb Mendel lay in his bed fully awake. He had wanted to recite the *Shema*, as he did every night, but he could not bring himself to pronounce the sacred words and all the more not the Divine Name. How could a vile sinner such as he was proclaim: "In thine hand, O Lord, I entrust my soul"? He had but one request of the Almighty: to let him be done with this world, its lusts, its temptations. What a bizarre transition: one moment he was poring over the sacred book, and an hour later he found himself ensnared in the net of incest. "It's a fall, a punishment," Reb Mendel murmured to himself. Somewhere he had read that temptations were sent to bedevil great saints

—like the Patriarch Abraham, or the Righteous Joseph—or else they were sent to the worst of sinners, putting them on the road to *Sheol*. That Lisa-Hadas had made him drunk, just as Lot's daughter had done to Lot. Well, and how did it happen that a brother of his, a son of God-fearing Jews, should take up with a Gentile woman and shame his parents in Paradise? And why had he deceived him, his older brother, and held back his money from him? Reb Mendel recalled the verse in the Book of Psalms: "And I, in my haste, cried out: 'All men are deceivers.'" Even a saint as King David had despaired of all mankind.

Yes, King David. He, the author of the Book of Psalms, had had his own share of troubles. One of his sons, Absalom, had plotted to seize the throne from his father and had openly copulated with ten of his father's wives. Another son, Amnon, had raped his sister, Tamar. Yet another, Adoniahu Ben Hagit, had sought to wrest the kingdom from his brother Solomon. And that event with Bathsheba and Uriah the Hittite! Well, but all these things belonged to ancient times. What did the Gemara say? "Whoever claims that David sinned is nothing but mistaken." Every word in the Holy Book was full of secrets.

Reb Mendel himself did not know who it was in his brain who spoke to him now: Satan or an angel of mercy? But of one thing he was sure: He needed to do penance. Even a brute like Nebuzaradan, a murderer of Jewish children: When later he regretted his deeds, Heaven accepted his atonement. But how could one atone for so heinous a deed as his, Mendel's, was? For the most trivial of sins the sacred book demanded hundreds of fasts, self-flagellations, rolling the body in the snow in the winter and in thorns in the summer. An abomination such as he had committed was not even mentioned in that holy book at all.

Reb Mendel was too restless to remain lying and so he sat up in his bed. Basha-Meitl awoke and asked him, "Mendel, aren't you sleeping?"

"No."

"Mendel, if what Lisa-Hadas told you is true then Joel stained the family's honor. But it is not your fault. The Patriarch Jacob also had a wicked brother: Esau."

"Yes, I know."

"Mendel, perhaps she lied? A woman like Lisa-Hadas is capable of bringing false accusations even against her own husband."

"No."

"Well, whatever happens—don't take it to heart. May God not punish me for saying this, but I never thought much of either one of them. I always told you that I had no faith in their honesty. But you ignored me, even scolded me. He stuffed his pockets with money and to you he doled out pennies. You know that is the truth."

"Go back to sleep."

"It will be a black day when word of this gets out in town."

"It's already a black day."

"When is he coming home?"

Reb Mendel didn't answer. He was reminded of the words in the Gemara: "Very good is death." That phrase had always puzzled him. The Torah was a teaching of life, not death. Only now did he understand what the words meant to say. Sometimes a man could become so hopelessly entangled that death was his only deliverance. And as if she could read his thoughts Basha-Meitl called out, "Take care of yourself. Your life comes before everything else. Good night."

Basha-Meitl fell silent, but apparently she was not asleep. A cricket which had lived for who knew how many years behind Basha-Meitl's stove suddenly began to chirp its eternal chirping; a creature who with one haunting note could say all that it had to say night in and night out, generation after generation. In a coop near the stove slept a hen and a rooster. Basha-Meitl was raising the pair to serve as sacrifices for herself and for Mendel on the eve of Yom Kippur. Every now and then the hen clucked in her sleep. Although Basha-Meitl and Mendel possessed a clock equipped with weights and chains which chimed precisely every hour and every half-hour, it was the rooster with his cockadoodledoo who awoke them every morning at the break of day. A kind of envy swept over Reb Mendel for those innocent creatures. True, the Almighty had not granted them free choice, but the turmoil of breaking His commandments also didn't trouble their days. They fulfilled their mission simply and faithfully.

Although he was convinced that the night was lost to sleep, Reb Mendel finally dozed off. He slept for several hours without dreaming, or perhaps without the memory of having dreamed. When he opened his eyes the room was still dark. He awoke with a heaviness in his heart and a bitter taste in his mouth. He remembered that some dreadful event had taken place, but what it was he couldn't say. "Why am I feeling so low?" he asked himself. "Have I wronged someone—or has someone wronged me?" Basha-

Meitl was sleeping now; he could hear her steady breathing. The cricket had stopped its chirping; perhaps it too had fallen asleep. Through the window Mendel saw the heavens thickly strewn with stars. He had once heard somewhere that each star was a complete world. So many worlds had the Almighty created that every righteous man was rewarded with three hundred and ten of them. Reb Mendel shivered. All at once he remembered the disaster that had befallen him in his old age.

Days and nights passed and Reb Mendel could not sleep. He would doze off, then wake up with a start. Although the nights in Lublin were quiet, his head throbbed with noise. Sometimes he heard the wheels of a carriage clattering across the cobblestones. Another time he heard a hammer striking loudly against an anvil. "Have I become another Titus that God should send a gnat to gnaw at my brain? Am I going mad?" Reb Mendel considered doing away with himself. But how? Should he hang himself? Drown? Take poison? Since he had already lost his share in the world to come, what was the difference what he did? In the midst of his turmoil Reb Mendel took pains to keep his condition from Basha-Meitl. But she saw it just the same and tried to comfort him. She pleaded with him: "Mendel, he is your brother, not your son. Even when a son strays from the righteous path one mustn't torment oneself."

Reb Mendel stopped going to pray with a quorum. He could not look the other Chassidim in the eye. He could not enter a sacred place where a Holy Ark stood filled with Torah scrolls. He put on his phylacteries in his study, but he could not bring himself to recite the benediction. He did not dare to kiss the fringes of his prayer shawl. Reb Mendel knew perfectly well that a Jew was forbidden to pray for death, but what, then, was left for him to do? He planned to leave a will requesting that he not be buried among those who died virtuous but behind the fence, where suicides and other sinful Jews lay buried.

On Fridays, like all other Jews, Reb Mendel used to go to the bathhouse, but no longer. How could he undress himself and bare to other Jews that organ, the sign of God's holy covenant, which had broken the injunction against incest? And how could he pray in the Chassidim-*shtibl*? What if he were called upon to read from the Torah? How could he pronounce the benediction over the Torah? Basha-Meitl informed the beadle of Przysucha that Mendel was ill and that he wanted no visitors.

In order to spare Basha-Meitl grief, Reb Mendel pretended to pray in his study. Friday evenings he put on his satin gaberdine and his fur-lined hat, he recited the "Woman of Valor," he blessed the wine—all in a hurry, without chants, without joy. He swallowed no more than two spoonfuls of the soup, touched neither the sweet stew nor the meat, barely tasted a morsel of challah. When Basha-Meitl asked why there was no singing of hymns at the Sabbath table, he said, "I don't feel like singing."

"Mendel, you've let yourself slip into melancholy. You are committing a sin."

"*Nu*, what's another sin?"

"Mendel, you frighten me."

"I won't make you suffer much longer," Reb Mendel said, against his will.

Twice a year, on Shavuot and then again on Rosh Hashanah, Reb Mendel was accustomed to travel to the *rebbe* in Przysucha. Although he was not a wealthy man, on those occasions he hired a coach and took along a number of the poorer Chassidim, those who could not afford the expenses of the trip. He paid for their lodgings in inns along the way, as well as their stay in Przysucha. The drive itself was one long celebration. The Chassidim crooned melodies, poked fun at the *Mitnagdim*, regaled each other with tales about the Rabbi of Lublin, the *Maggid* of Kozienice, Reb Melekh of Lizhensk, and about his brother Zusya. Reb Bunem was not an explicator of Torah, neither was he a miracle-worker. He did not accept payments for advice. He did not admit women into his study, and he did not give out amulets. On weekdays he did not wear a fur hat and a satin gaberdine, or even the white coat and trousers which Rabbi Menachem Mendel of Vitebsk and Rabbi Nachum of Tchernobil had worn. Instead, he went about in boots and a cloth coat, the same as the other Chassidim. But such was his greatness that scholars from every corner of Russian Poland had flocked to him, even from far-off Galicia. His disciples—Reb Yaakov of Radzymin, Yitzchak of Warka, Mendel of Kotzk, and Itche-Meir of Warsaw—were all about the same age as he, and each addressed him by the familiar "thou." They kidded him, and he in turn kidded them. They debated with him and good-naturedly contradicted him. Because few of Reb Bunem's Chassidim were elderly—mostly they were young—Reb Mendel of Lublin occupied a special place in Przysucha.

That year Reb Mendel startled the other Przysucha Chassidim in Lublin. Instead of waiting—as he had always done—for the week before Rosh Hashanah, he rented a carriage immediately after the first of Elul and departed for Przysucha alone, unaccompanied by other Chassidim. He did not even stop to take leave of anyone. "Did he suddenly become a miser?" the younger Chassidim wondered. "Was it a sudden show of arrogance?" Word of his illness had spread around the town, and it was concluded that that was the reason for his abrupt departure. Those Chassidim who could not afford to travel by carriage would have to travel on foot. Why all the fuss? If the Patriarch Jacob could hoof it all the way from Beer Sheba to Haran, healthy and young Chassidim could walk from Lublin to Przysucha.

It was a rare Chassid who arrived in Przysucha some three weeks before the holidays. Mendel was virtually alone. The large study house was empty. Unlike other men in his position, Reb Bunem was not one to require the services of a beadle or a *gabbai*. Mendel opened the door to the *rebbe*'s study and simply walked in. Reb Bunem—a tall man, with a pointed black beard and flashing black eyes—stood at a lectern and scribbled with a quill on a slip of paper. Seeing Reb Mendel, the *rebbe* wiped off his pen on his skullcap and asked, "Am I seeing things, or is my calendar wrong?"

"No, *Rebbe*. Your calendar is not wrong," Reb Mendel answered.

"*Nu*, welcome, welcome."

The rebbe stretched out his hand and Mendel barely touched the tips of his fingers, so as not to defile the saint's hand with his own. Reb Bunem threw a glance at him and knitted his brows. He moved a stool toward Reb Mendel and sat himself down on the edge of a bench. "Reb Mendel, what's troubling you? You may speak openly."

"*Rebbe*, I've forfeited my share in the world to come," Reb Mendel blurted out.

The *rebbe*'s eyes filled with laughter. "Forfeited, huh? Congratulations!"

"What does the *rebbe* mean?" Reb Mendel asked, alarmed.

"Those who pursue the world to come are engaged in a trade-off with the Almighty: 'I will observe your Torah and Commandments, and You'll give me a larger portion of the Leviathan.' When a Jew forfeits his share in the world to come, he can serve the Almighty for His own sake, expecting nothing in return."

"I am not worthy of serving Him," Reb Mendel said.

"And who, then, is worthy?"

Reb Mendel hoped that the *rebbe* would ask what he had done, and he was prepared to make a full confession. But the *rebbe* did not ask him. "He probably already knows," Reb Mendel thought to himself.

"Where are you staying?" Reb Bunem asked.

"I was given a bed in the inn. What more do I need?"

"Reb Mendel, take good care of yourself. The Master of the Universe has plenty of paid servants, but of those who would serve Him for nothing He has hardly any at all."

"*Rebbe*, I want to do penance."

"The wish itself is penance."

Reb Mendel wanted to say something more, but Reb

Bunem motioned with his hand as if to say: Enough for now. Before Mendel was out of the room, the *rebbe* called out to him, "Everything is permitted, except fasting!"

A fit of sobbing shook Mendel's body, and at the same time he was overcome with joy. He was not alone. The Almighty knew, and the *rebbe* also knew. He, Mendel, was sure to roast in the fires of all seven hells, but he also recalled a saying of the rebbe's: "Hell is for men, not for dogs." As long as there was a God and as long as there were Jews, what was the difference where one lived? Reincarnation? Let it be reincarnation. Purgatory? Let it be Purgatory. The *rebbe* had once said, "Among men there is justice and there is mercy. But for the Master of the Universe justice itself is mercy." Reb Mendel walked into the study house. Until that moment he had carefully avoided touching a holy book. He had not even dared to kiss the *mezuzah* with his unclean lips. But now he felt his strength returning to him. "No, I have no use for Paradise, I have no need for a reward." He walked up to the bookshelf and pulled down the tractate of *Berakhot*. He sat down all alone at a long table, and he began to chant the holy words and to interpret them to himself: "'At what time may one begin to recite the *Shema* in the evening? From the hour in which the priests gather to eat of their tithes.' Rashi had inserted an explanation: 'Priests who had become defiled and had immersed themselves in water. . . .'" Yes, Reb Mendel no longer hesitated to peruse the holy letters with which the Almighty had created the universe. A sinful Jew was still a

Jew. Even a convert, according to the Law, remained a Jew.

Days went by. Once again Reb Mendel was able to pray with fervor. It struck him that in all eighteen benedictions the prayers were written not for the individual Jew, but for the Jewish people as a whole. The plural form was used throughout. How could he, Mendel, pray for himself alone, for his own body, his own lost soul? But to pray for all the Jews—that, even the most wicked man on earth could do. Even the evil Balaam had been granted permission to praise the Jews and perhaps to pray for them.

Soon Reb Bunem's disciples and students from all over Poland began to gather. They were all there: Reb Mendel of Kotzk, Yaakov of Radzymin, Itche-Meir of Warsaw, Yitzchak of Warka, Mordecai Joseph of Izbica. Several of them had in the meantime themselves become rabbis, had students and followers of their own. Chassidim had also arrived from Lublin, some by horse and wagon, others on foot. Before Reb Mendel had hurried out of Lublin it had been rumored that he was gravely ill. Some of the Chassidim had believed that he had wanted to end his days with Reb Bunem in Przysucha. Now, Heaven be praised, he seemed to have come back to life. Although he had later on been given a private room at the inn, Reb Mendel had cots brought in for poor Lublin Chassidim who would otherwise have slept on a bench in the study house, in an attic somewhere, or wherever they could find a place to put down their heads. Reb Mendel paid for their meals as well.

Yes, once again Reb Mendel became what he had always been: a Chassid among Chassidim. It was thought that after the holidays he would return to Lublin, but Succot came and went and Reb Mendel was still in Przysucha. Somehow he learned that his brother Joel had converted and had gone off to live with a squire's wife. Lisa-Hadas had sold the shop without offering Basha-Meitl a share of the profits. Although according to the Law a Jew, even if he converted, remained a Jew, and although his wife could not remarry without a proper divorce, Lisa-Hadas married some "Enlightened" Jew, a lawyer by profession, and the man who had helped her to perpetrate her swindle. It was rumored that the two were living in some city deep in Russia. Reb Mendel wrote to Basha-Meitl informing her that he had made up his mind to stay in Przysucha and urging her to sell the house and join him there, because a wife's place was at her husband's side.

All these events unsettled and puzzled the Jews of Lublin, let alone the Przysucha Chassidim. That a Jew should fall in love with a Gentile and abandon Judaism was not unheard of. And besides, Joel had always been thought to be frivolous, a pleasure seeker. For a long time it had been whispered in Lublin that he made the rounds of the big cities far too often, more often than his business required, and that he hobnobbed too closely with Gentile landowners. But that a merchant, well-off as Reb Mendel had been, should forsake everything in order to sit at his *rebbe*'s feet —that was something new. Basha-Meitl traveled to Przysucha to persuade her husband to return with her to Lublin. "Is it your fault," she pleaded with him, "if your brother strayed from the righteous path?" But Reb Mendel was adamant: "It is written: 'All Jews are responsible one for the other.' If even perfect strangers share in this responsibility, how much more so should a brother?"

It took a good deal of argument before Basha-Meitl

agreed to settle in Przysucha. Miraculously she had managed to save up a small nest egg. She had also inherited several good pieces of jewelry from her mother, her grandmothers, and her great-grandmothers. She rented an apartment on Synagogue Street, not far from the *rebbe's* study house, and the couple began their new life. Reb Mendel did exactly what Reb Bunem told him to do: he served the Almighty without expecting any rewards. He rose at midnight, and he recited prayers and lamentations that had been printed in older prayer books. He prayed with fervor; he studied the Mishnah, the Gemara, other sacred texts. Although the *rebbe* had forbidden him to fast, Reb Mendel was fasting every Monday and Thursday. From the day he had sinned his appetite for food had diminished. He went to bed satiated and woke up feeling full. One meal in the morning, or in the evening instead, satisfied him. He no longer ate meat, except on the Sabbath. The *Reshit Chochmah* required those who committed a sin as grave as his to torture themselves and to fast from Sabbath to Sabbath. But Reb Mendel did not want to distress his wife. The truth was that she, Basha-Meitl, was also eating less and less, even though her household duties did not diminish. Of what little money the couple possessed they gave tithes. There was a small yeshiva in Przysucha and Basha-Meitl undertook to feed several of its students, to wash their linen, to patch up their socks and shirts. Reb Mendel never told her what had transpired between himself and his sister-in-law, but Basha-Meitl herself did not want to arrive at the world to come without good deeds to her credit.

As for Mendel, he did not occupy himself with thoughts of the world to come. True, it was far better to sit in Paradise with a crown on one's head and to bask in the glow of the Shechinah than to wallow in thorns or to turn into a worm, or a frog, or a monster. But the pleasures of living year round in Przysucha more than made up for the torment which might be his later. A day did not go by when the *rebbe* did not speak a few kind words to him. Merely to gaze upon the *rebbe*'s saintly countenance was an other-worldly joy. Rabbis and scholars flocked to Przysucha from Poland, from Volhynia, and occasionally from more distant lands as well. Reb Mendel became the *rebbe*'s *gabbai*, a service he performed without pay. When Reb Bunem was consulted on matters of commerce, worldly affairs, he always called Reb Mendel in and conferred with him. Reb Bunem himself was also well versed in those matters. It was no secret that he had once been an adherent of the Enlightenment, and a pharmacist. He himself was actually a penitent.

Why dream of Paradise when Przysucha itself was Paradise? Instead of being flung into the depths of *Sheol*, as he deserved to be, Reb Mendel was surrounded with Torah, with wisdom, with the love and the warmth of fellow Jews. Reb Mendel never spoke of his sin to Reb Bunem, but it was clear that through the divine spirit which rested on him the *rebbe* knew what he, Mendel, had done. Once, on Simchat Torah, when Reb Mendel was striding behind the *rebbe* with the Torah scroll in his arms, Reb Bunem suddenly stopped, turned back his head, and said, "Let the *Mitnaged* save up a nest egg for Paradise. We here in Przysucha are up to our necks in the glory of God and the radiance of the Torah right here and now."

Translated by Nili Wachtel

GIFTS

I met him near a bank where I cashed a check I received from a Yiddish newspaper. I was a young writer and he—I will call him Max Blendever—was known as a Zionist leader in Warsaw and a councilman in the city hall. He had quarreled with the major Zionist group and had become the head of a faction of extremists who called themselves revisionists. I recognized him from his pictures in the Yiddish press. He was of medium height, broad-shouldered, with a large head, high cheekbones, and thick eyebrows. I had noticed that politicians were inclined to let their eyebrows grow, most probably to appear more masculine or to hide their sly eyes. Max Blendever was known as a fighter. In the city council he assailed the anti-Semites violently. He had enemies not only among the Gentiles but also among the Jews who contended that he was too aggressive and did damage with his attacks.

As a rule, I would have never stopped a stranger in the street, especially not a famous man. But I had recently heard that this wife, Carola, had died in a car accident. This woman, whom I had never met, had sent me a New Year's card and a bottle of Carmel wine on the eve of Rosh Hashanah. The gift arrived at the address of the journal where I was a proofreader. It was a complete surprise to me. Was Carola Blendever a Yiddishist? Did she read me in the little magazines that never had more than a few hundred readers? As far as I knew, most of the wives of the Zionist leaders were half assimilated. I wanted to send the husband a condolence card when she passed away, but nothing ever came of it. I was one of those who considered him too arrogant. We Jews, I believed, should not forget that we are a minority in every country in the world, and should act accordingly.

But now that I encountered him face to face, I went over to him and said:

"You don't know me, but everyone knows you. My name is . . ."

"I know you, I heard of you," Max Blendever replied. He pulled out the cigar from between his lips, extended his hand to me, and shook mine vigorously. He said, "My late wife had mentioned your name once in a while. I am a politician, not a writer. Besides, I am for Hebrew, not for Yiddish, but I buy Yiddish books and journals. They are sent to me from time to time. In what direction are you walking? Perhaps you can accompany me a part of the way. You have certainly heard about the misfortune with my wife."

"Yes. I am terribly sorry. I had received a gift from her. I could not understand where she had heard about me and how I deserved it."

Max Blendever, who walked so quickly that I could barely keep up with him, suddenly stopped.

"A gift, huh? What sort of gift?"

"A bottle of Carmel wine."

Something like an angry smile appeared on his face. He measured me from head to toe. "You were not the only one," he said. "People have different passions. Some smoke opium, others take hashish. There are those whose greatest pleasure is to run in the forests and hunt bears or wolves. My Carola, may she rest in peace, had a passion for sending gifts. I was a poor boy when I married her, but she was a rich daughter. She received a handsome dowry and she spent it all on gifts."

We walked for a while in silence. Max Blendever took long strides. At Marshalkowski Street, he glanced around and said, "Now that I already began telling you about her, maybe you would like to go with me to a café? Let's drink a glass of coffee together."

"It would be an honor and a pleasure," I answered.

"What is the honor? Each of us does his own work, right or wrong. God will judge us if He exists. And if He doesn't exist, it is too bad. If you don't drink coffee, you can take a glass of tea, cocoa, or whatever you prefer. I like black coffee without cream or sugar."

We went to a café, and it was half empty in the middle of the day. A waiter came right over to our table. Max Blendever ordered black coffee for himself and tea with lemon for me. He re-lit his cigar with a lighter and said:

"Since you are a fiction writer, or plan to become one, you must be interested in people's character and their idiosyncrasies. I always knew that different types of philanthropists existed in the world. American millionaires give away fortunes for the most bizarre causes. One millionairess in Chicago, a spinster, left two million dollars to her poodle. But my Carola's passion to send gifts, often to complete strangers, was something new to me. She never told me about them, although I heard her speak about various presents. I thought this was the way rich women behaved. With them, every emotion must be expressed in concrete terms. Having had little experience with the so-called beautiful sex, I left her to her own devices. You are looking at a man who never had another woman aside from his lawful wife. For me, affairs were only a waste of time. I had the illusion that all females were more or less alike."

"If only I could have such an illusion," I said.

"Huh? My real passion was politics. It began when I was still a boy. From childhood on, I always heard Jews lamenting about their fate to live in Exile. I thought to myself: 'What can come from all this moaning and sighing? Why not do something?' And this is how I became what I am today. My father taught me that a Jew must bow his head when people abuse him and offer the other cheek. This was sheer nonsense to me. But let me return to my story. Maybe you could even write about it someday, but don't mention my name."

"I certainly wouldn't."

"Yes, my wife. I had, as they say, one God and one wife. I loved her and believe she loved me too. But her mania of sending gifts had always baffled me. Of course she also had a buying mania. You cannot give gifts without buying them first. I sometimes think that her drive to buy things was her passion number one. I could never take a walk with her. She was forever window-shopping. Once, we were walking in the vicinity of the Catholic cemetery in Powazek. We passed a store which displayed coffins and sure enough she stopped to stare at them. I asked her, 'Do you want to buy a coffin? You know that Jews don't bury their dead in coffins, at least not here in Poland.' But you could not tear her away from a store window. I tell you this to show how compulsive her buying mania was. I discovered about her obsession for gifts later. Let me make it short. Every year she sent gifts to hundreds of men, women, and children. She only waited for an excuse to celebrate some event, a holiday, a birthday, an engagement party, a wedding, a circumcision, you name it. I found a notebook where she listed countless candidates and occasions for her benefactions. She had virtually given away her entire inheritance. As you can imagine, I was often on the road—congresses, conferences, an endless number of party meetings. You know our Jewish organizations. Every party has its factions, and sooner or later every faction splits. Here in Warsaw we have a leftist politician, a certain Dr. Bruk, who has already been everything in his life: a Bundist, a communist, a member of the right Labor Zionists, the left Labor Zionists, an anarchist, a Sejmist, a Territorialist. His last party had split so many times until it became a faction of a faction of a faction. A joke is told that when his present remnant of a party decides to hold a general meeting, instead of a hall they hire a *droshky* pulled by a single horse.

"Needless to say, a man with my temperament and my big mouth has no lack of enemies. It cannot be any other way. But in the last few years I began to realize that my enemies had somehow become more lenient than they used to be. Even when they attacked me, they did it, so to say, with kid gloves. Their arguments were mollified with bits of praise. Here and there they even pointed out some of my merits. 'What happened? Why have they become so charitable towards me?' I wondered. 'Do they consider me so old and far gone that I am altogether harmless? Or have my opponents grown slightly civilized in their old age?' I was too busy to ponder it. Yes, you guessed it! Carola had decided that I didn't have enough friends for her barrage of gifts and began sending presents to my enemies.

"When I found out about it I raised hell. It was the first and last time I spoke about divorce. I knew none of my enemies could ever have believed that Carola had done all this without my knowledge. They were all convinced that the wolf had become a lamb and decided to pad his career with bribery. I screamed so that our neighbors came running. My wife had entirely destroyed the little reputation I had built up in a lifetime. She had completely ruined me. How do they say it? A thousand enemies cannot do more harm to a man than a well-meaning wife can do. I say well-meaning because when my anger had subsided (how long can someone rage and break plates?) and I tried to explain to her what a catastrophe all this was for me, she swore that she could not understand why I made such a fuss. She was saying, 'What is so terrible about showing a little good will? Your enemies actually have the same goal as you: to help the Jews. It is only that their approach is different.'

"My dear young man, I don't know myself why I'm confiding all this to you. Until now, I haven't told it to anyone. After brooding over it a long time and eating my heart out, I made peace with the fact that the damage was done. What could I do? Write letters to all my adversaries explaining that my wife sent them gifts without my consent? I would only make myself ridiculous. I decided to do what I believed was my duty and that what my enemies think of me or say did not matter. I can only tell you that out of all the gifts the bottle of wine she sent to you was the most sensible. You are a young writer and have nothing to do with politics. But to send a Christmas gift to the greatest anti-Semite in Poland—Adam Nowaczynski—is absolutely an act that borders on madness."

"She did this?" I asked.

"Yes, exactly. The irony of it is that this deranged Jew-baiter wrote her an exceptionally friendly letter where he praised the Jews to Heaven. He wrote, more or less, that he maligns the Jews only because he knows how intelligent they are, what sharp minds they have developed by study-ing the Talmud, and how dangerous their competition is for the naïve and gullible Poles who can be outsmarted so easily. Let us find a way to utilize our respective potentials for the common good of all Polish citizens, and so on and so on. Like all demagogues, he believed his own lies."

"Giving presents is not something new in our history," I said. "When Jacob heard that his brother Esau was com-ing to meet him with four hundred armed ruffians, he sent a gift which would have been worth a treasure today."

"Yes. Yes. Yes. The weaker ones always try to curry favor, but it doesn't help for long," Max Blendever said. "They take what you give them, embrace you, kiss you, call you brother, and a little later they assault you again. The truth is that Carola did this not to help the Jews. It was nothing but her addiction to gifts. Freud would have interpreted it with hair-splitting casuistry, most probably with some newly discovered gift complex. He and his disciples must rationalize every sort of human peculiarity. But in what lousy book is it written that everything can be explained? My theory is that nothing can be explained."

"This is also my theory," I said. "When literature goes too far into explanations and commentaries, it becomes tedious and false."

"Yes, right," Max Blendever agreed. "Your tea has gotten cold. Should I order for you a glass of hot tea?"

"Thank you, no. Definitely not."

"Why not?" Max Blendever asked and I replied:

"This can never be explained."

Translated by Deborah Menashe

— יאָ, יאָ, יאָ. דאָס טוען אַלע שוואַכע, אָבער
ס׳העלפֿט נישט אויף לאַנג — האָט מאַקס בלענדעווער
געזאָגט. — זיי נעמען צו די מתנה, קושן דיך, רופֿן דיך
ברודער, און אַ ביסל שפּעטער העצן זיי שוין ווידער. אמת
אָדער נישט?

— יאָ, אמת.

— דער אמת איז אַז קאַראַלאַ האָט דאָס נישט געטאָן
צו העלפֿן ייִדן. ס׳איז איינפֿאַך געווען איר דראַנג אָדער
צוואַנג פֿאַר מתנות — האָט מאַקס בלענדעווער געזאָגט.

— פֿרויד וואָלט נאַטירלעך געהאַט דערוועגן וואָס צו
דערשענען. ער און די תלמידים זײַנע האָבן אַיין פֿאַרלאַנג:
צו ראַציאָנאַליזירן די מענטשלעכע לײַדנשאַפֿטן. זיי מוזן
געפֿינען אויף אַלץ אַן אויפֿקלערונג. אָבער אין וואָסער
ספֿר פּראָלניק שטייט עס געשריבן אַז אַלץ האָט אַן
אויפֿקלערונג? מײַן טעאָריע איז אַז קיין שום זאַך קאָן
קיינער נישט אויפֿקלערן.

— ס׳איז אויך מײַן טעאָריע — האָב איך געזאָגט —
ווען ליטעראַטור לאָזט זיך אַרײַן אין אויפֿקלערונגען און
קאָמענטאַרן ווערט זי פֿאַלש און לאַנגווײַליק.

— אַזוי? יאָ, ריכטיק — האָט מאַקס בלענדעווער
אײַנגעשטימט. — אײַער קאַווע איז קאַלט. זאָל איך
באַשטעלן פֿאַר אײַך אַ גלאָז הייסע קאַווע?

— ניין, אַבסאָלוט נישט.

פֿאַר וואָס נישט? — האָט מאַקס בלענדעווער
געפֿרעגט און איך האָב געענטפֿערט:

— דאָס קאָן קיינער נישט אויפֿקלערן.

עסעגיש בין איך געקומען צום באַשלוס אַז איך קאָן
גאָרנישט פֿאַרריכטן. וואָס האָב איך געקאָנט טאָן? שרײַבן
בריוו צו מײַנע שׂונאים אַז די מתּנות האָט מײַן ווײַב
געשיקט אָן מײַן וויסן? איך וואָלט מיך בלויז געמאַכט
לעכערלעך. איך האָב מיר געזאָגט: דו טו וואָס דו
האַלטסט ס׳איז דײַן פֿליכט און וואָס דײַנע שׂונאים
טראַכטן וועגן דיר אָדער רעדן וועגן דיר איז נישט
וויכטיק. אײַן זאַך וויל איך אײַך זאָגן: פֿון אַלע מתּנות
וואָס זי האָט געשיקט איז די פֿלאַש ווײַן וואָס איר האָט
דערהאַלטן געוון די סאַמע געוווּנטשנסטע. איר זענט אַ
יונגער שרײַבער, איר האָט גאָרנישט צו טאָן מיט פּאָליטיק.
אָבער שיקן אַ נײַיאָר־מתּנה דעם גרעסטן פּוילישן
אַנטיסעמיט, נאָוואַטשינסקין, — דאָס איז שוין עפּעס וואָס
האָט מיך שׁיער נישט געטריבן צו משוגעת.

— דאָס וואָס זי האָט געטאָן? — האָב איך געפֿרעגט.

— יאָ, גענוי דאָס. דאָס קאָמישסטע איז וואָס דער
דאָזיקער מאַניאַק און ייִדן־פֿרעסער האָט איר אָנגעשריבן
אַ זעלטן פֿרײַנטלעכן בריוו. ער האָט אין דעם בריוו
געלויבט ייִדן אין הימל אַרײַן. ער האָט געשריבן מער־
ווייניקער אַז ער קעמפֿט קעגן ייִדן דערפֿאָר דערפֿאַר ווײַל ער
ווייסט ווי אינטעליגענט זיי זענען, וואָסערע שאַרפֿע מוחות
זיי האָבן פֿון שטודירן דעם תּלמוד און ווי געפֿערלעך
זייער קאָנקורענץ איז פֿאַר די נאַיִווע פּאָלאַקן וואָס גלויבן
יעדן אויפֿן וואָרט, לאָזן זיך אויסנוצן פֿון יעדן איינעם און
אַזוי ווײַטער. ער האָט, ווײַזט־אויס, געגלויבט אין זײַנע
אייגענע שקרים.

— געבן מתּנות איז נישט עפּעס קיין נײַעס בײַ ייִדן —
האָב איך געזאָגט. — ווען יעקבֿ אָבֿינו האָט געהערט אַז זײַן
ברודער עשׂו גייט אים אַקעגן מיט פֿיר הונדערט
באַוואָפֿנטע כּוליגאַנעס האָט ער אים אַקעגנגעפֿירט אַ
מתּנה וואָס וואָלט הײַנט געוון ווערט אַן אוצר.

מײַן קאַראַלאַ האָט אײַנגעזען אַז איך האָב נישט גענוג
פֿרײַנד פֿאַר דעם מבול פֿון אירע מתנות און אָנגעהויבן
שיקן מתנות מײַנע שׂונאים.

ווען איך האָב מיך דאָס דערוווּסט האָב איך געמאַכט
אַ מוראדיקן סקאַנדאַל. דאָס איז געווען דאָס ערשטע און
לעצטע מאָל ווען איך האָב גענומען רעדן וועגן אַ גט. יענע
וואָס האָבן געקראַגן די מתנות וואָלטן קיין מאָל נישט
געגלויבט אַז קאַראַלאַ האָט עס געטאָן אָן מײַן וויסן. זיי
זענען אַלע געווען זיכער אַז דער וואָלף איז געוואָרן אַ
לעמעלע און אַז איך האָב באַשלאָסן אונטערצוצעטן מײַן
קאַרריערע מיט קאַבער. איך האָב יענעם טאָג געמאַכט
אַזוינע געוואַלדן אַז די שכנים זענען זיך צונויפֿגעלאָפֿן.
מײַן ווײַב האָט געהאַט חרוֹבֿ געמאַכט דאָס גאַנצע ביסל
פּרעסטיזש וואָס איך האָב אויפֿגעבויט אין אַ לעבן. זי האָט
מיך פֿולשטענדיק רויִנירט. ווי זאָגט מען עס? טויזנט
שׂונאים קאַנען ניט טאָן אַ מענטש דאָס שלעכטס וואָס ער
טוט זיך אַלײן. טויזנט שׂונאים קאַנען אים נישט אַזוי
קאַמפּראָמיטירן און פֿאַרשעמען וויפֿל אַ ווײַב קאָן דאָס
טאָן אומשולדיקערהייט. איך זאָג אומשולדיקערהייט ווײַל
ווען מײַן גמיט האָט זיך אַ קאַפּעלע אײַנגעשטילט — ווי
לאַנג קאָן מען שטורמען און שרײַען און ברעכן טעלער?
— און איך האָב געפֿרווװט איר געבן צו פֿאַרשטיין וואָס
פֿאַר אַ קאַטאַסטראָפֿע דאָס איז פֿאַר מיר, האָט זי
געשווירן אַז זי קאָן נישט באַגרײַפֿן פֿאַר וואָס איך מאַך
אַזאַ טומל. זי האָט געטענהט: וואָס איז דאָס אַזאַ עוולה אַז
מ׳ווײַזט אַרויס מענטשן אַ ביסל גוטן ווילן? די אַלע
שׂונאים דײַנע ווילן דאָס אייגענע וואָס דו: העלפֿן ייִדן.
נישט מער, זיי האָבן אַנדערע מעטאָדן. מײַן ליבער
יונגערמאַן, איך ווייס אַליין נישט פֿאַר וואָס איך דערצייל
אײַך דאָס אַלץ. איך האָב ביז איצט דאָס קיינעם נישט
דערצײַלט. נאָר לאַנגע טראַכטעגישן און אַ סך האַרץ־

אַװעק אַ װאָר איך זאָל נישט מוזן ערגעץ פֿאַרן: אַ
קאָנגרעסן, קאָנפֿערענצן, אומצאָליקע פֿאַרזאַמלונגען,
מיטינגען. איר קאָנט אונזערע יִידישע אָרגאַניזאַציעס.
יעדע פּאַרטיי האָט אירע פֿראַקציעס און אין יעדער
פֿראַקציע קומט פֿאָר פֿריִער אָדער שפּעטער אַ
שפּאַלטונג. מיר האָבן דאָ אין װאַרשע איינעם אַ דאָקטער
ברוק און ער איז שוין אַלץ געװוען אין זײַן לעבן: אַ
בונדיסט, אַ קאָמוניסט, אַ מאַכער בײַ די רעכטע פּועלי־
ציון, בײַ די לינקע פּועלי־ציון, אַן אַנאַרכיסט, אַ סיימיסט,
אַ טעריטאָריאַליסט, אַ פֿאַראייניקטער. די לעצטע פּאַרטיי
זײַנע האָט זיך אַזױ פֿיל מאָל געשפּאָלטן ביז ס׳איז געבליבן
אַ פֿראַקציע פֿון אַ פֿראַקציע. ס׳גייט אַרום אַ װיץ אַז װען
די פּאַרטיי זײַנע באַשליסט צו האָבן אַן אַלגעמיינע
פֿאַרזאַמלונג און זיי קאָנען נישט קריגן קיין לאָקאַל, דינגען
זיי אַ דראָשקע. ס׳איז אַ װיץ, אָבער ס׳איז נישט װײַט פֿון
אמת.

איר װייסט אַװודאי אַז איך האָב אָן אַ שיעור שׂונאים
און ס׳קאָן נישט זײַן אַנדערש בײַ אַ מענטש מיט מײַן
טעמפּעראַמענט און מײַן מויל. די לעצטע פֿאַר יאָר איז
מיר אויפֿגעפֿאַלן אַז עפּעס זענען די שׂונאים מײַנע געװאָרן
צו מיר אַ סך מילדער װי זיי זענען געװען. אַפֿילו װען זיי
אַטאַקירן מיך, טוען זיי דאָס, װי מ׳זאָגט, דורך זײַדענע
הענטשקעס. זיי פֿאַלעמיזירן מיט מיר, אָבער דערבײַ
װאַרפֿן זיי מיר צו דאָ און דאָרט אַ קאָמפּלימענט און װײַזן
אָן אויף מײַנע פֿאַרדינסטן. װאָס איז געשען? האָב איך מיך
געבֿרעגט. האָלט מען שױן אַז איך אַז בין אַזױ אַלט און
אָפּגעפֿאָרן אַז איך בין שױן אין גאַנצן אומשעדלעך? אָדער
זענען אונזערע פּאַרטייִישע קאַלבלעפֿל געװאָרן אַ קאַפּעלע
מער ציװיליזירט? איך בין צו פֿיל פֿאַרנומען צו קאָנען זיך
לאַנג גריבלען אין אַזױנע ענינים. יאָ, איר האָט געטראָפֿן.

אײַך דערצײלן. דאָס קאָן אײַך אַמאָל צונוץ קומען אין אײַער שרײַבן, נאָר רופֿט נישט אָן מײַן נאָמען.

— נײן.

— יאָ, מײַן װײַב. איך האָב געהאַט, װי מ׳זאָגט, אײן גאָט און אײן װײַב. איך האָב זי ליב געהאַט און איך גלױב אַז זי האָט מיך אױך ליב געהאַט. אָבער דאָס געבן מתּנות האָט מיט דער צײַט פֿאַרנומען איר גאַנצן מוח. זי האָט אױך געהאַט אַ קױפֿמאַניע. מתּנות מוז מען קױפֿן. טײל מאָל טראַכט איך אַז דאָס געבן מתּנות האָט זיך אַנטװיקלט פֿון איר מאַניע צו קױפֿן. איך האָב קײן מאָל נישט געקאָנט גײן מיט איר שפּאַצירן. זי האָט זיך בוכשטעבלעך אָפּגעשטעלט בײַ יעדן שױפֿענצטער. אײן מאָל איז מיר אױסגעקומען צו זײַן מיט איר אין פֿאַװאָנזעק נעבן דעם צמענטאַר(*) און מיר זענען פֿאַרבײַ אַ געשעפֿט פֿון טרומנעס. זי האָט גלײַך געטאָן דאָס איריקע: זיך אָפּגעשטעלט און געגומען גלאָצן אױף די טרומנעס. כ׳פֿרעג זי: װילסט קױפֿן אַ טרומנע? ייִדן באַגראַבט מען נישט אין קײן טרומנעס, און דו װײסט עס גאַנץ װױל. נישט בײַ אונדז אין פּױלן. איך דערצײל עס אײַך בלױז דערפֿאַר צו װײַזן װי שטאַרק ס׳איז געװען בײַ איר די קױפֿמאַניע. װעגן די מתּנות האָב איך זיך דערװוּסט שפּעטער.

לאָמיך עס מאַכן בקיצור. זי האָט געשיקט יעדעס יאָר מתּנות הונדערטער מענטשן, מאַנסלײַט און פֿרױען. זי האָט נײַערט געזוכט אַ געלעגנהייט: אַ יום־טובֿ, אַ געבורטסטאָג, אַ תּנאָים, אַ חתונה, אַ ברית. איך האָב געפֿונען בײַ איר אַ בוך װוּ זי האָט געהאַט פֿאַרשריבן צענדליקער בלעטער מיט נעמען און דאַטעס פֿון דערװאַקסענע און קינדער. זי האָט פֿאַקטיש אױסגעגעבן דערױף איר גאַנצע ירושה. איך בין אָפֿט געװען אונטערװוועגנס. די לעצטע יאָרן איז נישט

* Gentile cemetery.

פֿאַרשיידנסטע צוועקן. אײן מיליאָנערשע, אַן אַלטע מויד, האָט איבערגעלאָזט איר הונט אַ מיליאָן דאָלאַר. איך וווּנדער זיך נישט ווען איך לייען דערוועגן. יעדער אײנער האָט זײַנע משוגעתן, קאַפּריזן. אָבער מײַן קאָראָלאָס תאווה צו געבן מתּנות, אָפֿט צו ווילד פֿרעמדע מענטשן, איז געווע‌ן פֿאַר עפּעס נײַ. איך האָב דאָס נישט אַנטדעקט בײַ איר מיט אַ מאָל. איך האָב זי אָפֿט געהערט רעדן וועגן מתּנות, אָבער איך האָב געמיינט אַז אַזוי פֿירט זיך צווישן די רײַכע און ספּעציעל בײַם ווײַבערשן מין. בײַ זיי מוזן זיך אַלע געפֿילן אויסדריקן קאָנקרעט. אויב מען טוט זיי אַ געפֿעליקייט, צאָלן זיי צוריק מיט אַ מתּנה. איך האָב ווייניק געהאַט צו טאָן מיט דעם שיינעם געשלעכט ביז צו דער חתונה און דער אמת איז אַז אויך נישט צו פֿיל נאָך דער חתונה. איך בין אויף מײַן שטייגער שרעקלעך אַלטמאָדיש. דאָ פֿאַר אײַך זיצט אַ מאַנסביל וואָס האָט קיין מאָל נישט געהאַט קיין אַנדער פֿרוי אַחוץ זײַן געזעצלעכער ווײַב. נישט איך האָב געהאַט צײַט דערצו און נישט דאָס גרױדאלד, איך האָב די אילוזיע, אַז אַלע ווײַבער זענען אין גרונט די זעלבע.

— הלוואַי וואָלט איך געקאָנט האָבן אַזאַ אילוזיע — האָב איך געזאָגט.

— האַ? מײַן לייַדנשאַפֿט איז פּאָליטיק. ס׳האָט זיך אָנגעהויבן בײַ מיר ווען איך בין נאָך געווען אַ ייִנגל. איך האָב פֿון קינדווײַז אָן געהערט קרעכצן אויפֿן גורל פֿון ייִדן און איך האָב בײַ מיר געטראַכט: וואָס קאָן אַרויסקומען פֿון די אַלע קרעכצעניש אין זיפֿצעניש? פֿאַר וואָס נישט עפּעס טאָן? און אַזוי בין איך געוואָרן דאָס וואָס איך בין. מײַן טאַטע האָט מיך געלערנט אַז אַ ייִד דאַרף אײַנבויגן דעם קאָפּ ווען מען זידלט אים און געבן די אַנדערע באַק ווען מען שלאָגט אים, אָבער איך האָב דאָס נישט געוואָלט הערן. לאָמיך בעסער זיך אומקערן צו דעם וואָס איך וויל

מיר זענען געגאַנגען אַ צײַט שווײַגנדיקערהייט. מאַקס
בלענדעוועער האָט געמאַכט לאַנגע און גיכע שפּאַן. ס׳איז
געווען עפּעס פֿון אַ מיליטער־מאַן אין דעם דאָזיקן מענטש.
מיר זענען אַרויסגעקומען אויף דער מאַרשאַלקאַווסקע־גאַס
און ער האָט זיך ווידער אָפּגעשטעלט און גענומען זיך
אומקוקן רעכטס, לינקס. ער האָט געזאָגט:
— ווי באַלד איך האָב אײַך שוין אָנגעהויבן דערציילן
וועגן איר, אפֿשר וועלט איר אַרײַנגיין מיט מיר אין אַ
קאַפֿע? לאָמיר טרינקען אַ גלאָז קאַווע צוזאַמען.
— ס׳וואָלט געווען פֿאַר מיר אַ כּבֿוד און אַ פֿאַרגעניגן
— האָב איך געענטפֿערט.
— וואָס איז דער כּבֿוד? יעדער פֿון אונדז טוט דאָס
זײַניקע, גוט אָדער שלעכט. זאָל גאָט מישפּטן אויב ער
עקזיסטירט, און אויב ער עקזיסטירט נישט, איז אויך
פֿאַרפֿאַלן. אויב איר טרינקט נישט קיין קאַווע, קאָנט איר
נעמען אַ גלאָז טיי, קאַקאַאָ, אָדער וואָס איר ווילט. איך
האָב ליב שוואַרצע קאַווע, אָן שמאַנט און אָן צוקער. אָט
איז אַ קאַפֿע.
מיר זענען אַרײַן אין אַ קאַפֿע וואָס איז איצט, אין
מיטן טאָג געווען ליידיק. מיר האָבן זיך אַוועקגעזעצט בײַ
אַ טיש אין אַ ווינקל. מאַקס בלענדעווערס ציגאַר איז
געהאַט אויסגעגאַנגען און ער האָט אים ווידער אָנגעצונדן
מיט אַ צינד־מאַשינדל. אַ קעלנער איז גלײַך צוגעקומען.
מאַקס בלענדעוועער האָט באַשטעלט שוואַרצע קאַווע פֿאַר
זיך און קאַווע מיט מילך פֿאַר מיר. ער האָט געזאָגט:
— ווי באַלד איר זענט אַ בעלעטריסט, אָדער איר
גרייט זיך דאָס צו זײַן, מוזט איר זײַן אינטערעסירט אין
מענטשלעכע כאַראַקטערן און אידיאָסינקראַציעס. איך האָב
אַלע מאָל געוווּסט אַז ס׳זענען פֿאַראַן פֿילאַנטראָפֿן אויף
דער וועלט. טייל אַמעריקאַנער מיליאָנערן אָדער
מיליאַרדערן האָבן אַוועקגעגעבן אוצרות פֿאַר די סאַמע

— איך בין אַ פּאָליטיקער נישט אַ שרײַבער. איך בין
פֿאַר העברעיִש, נישט פֿאַר ייִדיש, אָבער איך קויף ייִדישע
ביכער און זשורנאַלן. מען שיקט זיי מיר צו סיײַ-ווי-סיַײ.
מײַן גאָטזעליקע פֿרוי האָט אַ פֿאַר מאָל דערמאָנט אײַער
נאָמען. אין וואָס פֿאַר אַ ריכטונג גייט איר? קומט מיט
מיר. באַגלייט מיך אַ שטיקל וועגס. אַזוי, איר האָט אַוודאי
געהערט פֿון דעם אומגליק מיט מײַן פֿרוי.

— יאָ צום באַדויערן, איך האָב אויף ראש-השנה
באַקומען פֿון איר אַ פּרעכטיקע ווינטשקאַרטע און אַ
מתנה. כ׳קאָן נישט באַגרײַפֿן פֿון וואַנען זי האָט געוווּסט
וועגן מיר און ווי אַזוי איך האָב דאָס פֿאַרדינט —
מאַקס בלענדעוער, וואָס איז געגאַנגען גיך, מיט אַזאַ
אימפּעט אַז איך האָב אים קוים געקאָנט נאָכפֿאַלגן, האָט
זיך פּלוצים אָפּגעשטעלט.

— אַ מתנה, האַ? וואָס פֿאַר אַ מתנה?
— אַ פֿלאַש כּרמל-ווײַן.

אויף זײַן פּנים האָט זיך באַוויזן עפּעס אַזוינס ווי אַ
בייזער שמייכל. ער האָט מיך אָפּגעמאָסטן פֿון אויבן
אַראָפּ, פֿון אונטן אַרויף און געזאָגט:

— קומט. איר זענט נישט געוווען בײַ איר דער
איינציקער. ס׳זענען פֿאַראַן פֿאַרשיידענע לײַדנשאַפֿטן בײַ
מענטשן. טייל רויכערן אָפּיום, אַנדערע נעמען חאַשיש;
פֿאַראַן אַזוינע וואָס זייער גרעסטער פֿאַרגעניגן איז
אַרומצולויפֿן איבער די ביאַלאַביעזשער וועלדער מיט אַ
ביקס און שיסן בערן, אָדער זשוברעס. מײַן קאַראַלאַ, רוען
זאָל זי אין ליכטיקן גן-עדן, האָט געהאַט אַ לײַדנשאַפֿט צו
שיקן מתנות. איך בין געווען אַן אָרעמער בחור ווען איך
האָב מיט איר חתונה געהאַט, אָבער זי איז געווען אַ
גבֿירישע טאָכטער. זי האָט אַפֿילו געקראָגן אַ היפּשן נדן
הגם איך האָב דאָס נישט פֿאַרלאַנגט, און אַלץ איז אַרײַן
אין מתנות.

אַגרעסיוו און אַז ער ברענגט שאָדן מיט זײַנע אַטאַקעס.
געוויינלעך וואָלט איך נישט אָפּגעשטעלט עמעצן וואָס
קאָן מיך נישט אין גאַס און באַזונדערס אַ באַרימטן
מענטש. אָבער איך האָב געהערט מיט אַ פּאָר וואָכן פֿריִער
אַז זײַן פֿרוי, קאַראָלאַ, איז געהאַט אומגעקומען אין אַ
קאַר־צוזאַמענשטויס. צוליב עפּעס וואָס איך האָב נישט
פֿאַרשטאַנען, האָט די דאָזיקע פֿרוי, וואָס איך האָב קיין
מאָל נישט באַגעגנט, מיר געהאַט געשיקט ערב ראָש־השנה
אַ ווונטשקאַרטע און אַ פֿלאַש כּרמל־ווײַן. די מתּנה איז
אָנגעקומען אויפֿן אַדרעס פֿון אַ ליטעראַרישן זשורנאַל וווּ
איך בין געווען אַ קאָרעקטאָר. די דאָזיקע מתּנה האָט מיך
גרײַעלעך פֿאַרווּנדערט. איז קאַראָלאַ בעלענדעוווער געווען אַ
ייִדישיסטין? האָט זי מיך געלייענט אין די קליינע
זשורנאַלעבלעך וואָס האָבן קיין מאָל נישט געהאַט מער ווי
עטלעכע הונדערט לייענערס? אויף ווי ווײַט איך האָב
געוווּסט זענען די ווײַבער פֿון די ציוניסטישע מנהיגים אַלע
געווען האַלב אַסימילירט. ווען איך האָב דערהערט אַז זי
איז אומגעקומען האָב איך געוואָלט שיקן דעם מאַן אַ
קאַנדאָלענץ־בריוו אָבער עפּעס איז נישט געקומען דערצו.
איך האָב אַליין אויך געהערט צו יענע וואָס האָבן
געהאַלטן אַז מאַקס בעלענדעוווער האָט צו פֿיל חוצפּה. מיר
ייִדן האָבן נישט געטאָרט פֿאַרגעסן אַז מיר זענען אַ
מינדערהייט אין אַלע לענדער פֿון דער וועלט.
איצט אַז איך האָב אים באַגעגנט פּנים־אל־פּנים, בין
איך צוגעגאַנגען צו אים און געזאָגט:
— איר קאָנט מיך נישט, אָבער אַלע קאָנען אײַך. מײַן
נאָמען איז — —
— כ׳קאָן אײַך, כ׳וווייס פֿון אײַך — האָט מאַקס
בעלענדעוווער אַ רוף געטאָן. ער האָט אַרויסגעכאַפּט דעם
ציגאַר פֿון צווישן די ליפּן, מיר דערלאַנגט אַ שטאַרקע
האַנט און געטאָן אַ פֿעסטן דריק. ער האָט געזאָגט:

מתנות

א

איך האָב אים געטראָפֿן נעבן א באַנק ווו איך בין
אַוועק אויסבײַטן אַ טשעק וואָס איך האָב געקראָגן פֿון אַ
ייִדישער צײַטונג. איך בין געווען אַ יונגער שרײַבער, און
ער, מאַקס בלענדעווער, אַ באַקאַנטער ציוניסטישער פֿירער
אין וואַרשע און אַ ראַטסמאַן אין שטאָטראַט. ער האָט זיך
געהאַט צעקריגט מיט די אַלגעמיינע ציוניסטן און איז
געוואָרן אַ טוער בײַ אַ פֿראַקציע פֿון עקסטרעמיסטן, די
אַזויגערופֿענע רעוויזיאָניסטן. איך האָב אים דערקענט פֿון
זײַנע בילדער אין די ייִדישע צײַטונגען: נישט הויך,
ברייטבייניק, מיט אַ גרויסן קאָפ פֿאַר אײַנעם פֿון זײַן
ווּקס, מיט הויכע קינבאָקן און מיט געדיכטע ברעמען־
בערשטעלעך. איך האָב שוין לאַנג געהאַט אײַנגעזען אַז
פּאָליטיקער האָבן אַ נייגונג צו לאָזן וואָקסן די ברעמען,
אַזוי אין פּוילן און אַזוי אין אַנדערע לענדער. האָבן זיי
דאָס געטאָן זיך צוצוגעבן מער מענלעכקייט, אָדער צו
פֿאַרדעקן די אויגן מ׳זאָל נישט אַרויסזען זייערע שלויע
שטיק? מאַקס בלענדעווער איז געווען באַקאַנט פֿאַר
איינעם מיט אַ קעמפֿערישער נאַטור. ער האָט געהאַלטן
אין שטאָטראַט שאַרפֿע רעדעס קעגן די אַנטיסעמיטן. ער
האָט געהאַט שונאים נישט בלויז צווישן די גויים, נאָר
אויך צווישן ייִדן וואָס האָבן געטענהט אַז ער איז צו

מתנות 🌿